WHATEVER HAPPENED TO MY EX
A Heartfelt Romantic Comedy

D1518316

POPPY CARTER

ONE

I dodge between the parked film equipment trucks, balancing five smoothies that have all been wedged into one of those cardboard trays made for four drinks. Rupert, the high-maintenance and extremely talented director, has requested a raw cacao beetroot ginger, since today we are shooting close to his favorite juice bar in all of Manhattan. As soon as I said, "Oh, I'll go!" some around camera (cinematographer, script supervisor, and the two actors) jumped on the cold-pressed organic bandwagon. I really don't mind going, but I just hope Maria, my stressed-out boss, doesn't find out that I left the set to get smoothies. She's all about *that's-not-your-job-Carly* but I'm all about *how-can-I-help-everybody* because I want job security and hey, I just like to help out. And that means I'd better get these BPA-free plastic cups that are sweating under the spring sunshine to set as soon as possible.

POPPY CARTER

The set decorator is unloading a heavy table from one of the trucks, and since it's on my way, I grab one side of it with my free hand to help her. She has a couple of chairs that need to come out of the truck as well, so I set down my drink tray and pitch in. The more I make myself useful, the more needed I am. A film crew is kind of like a big family — everyone needs to pitch in wherever they can.

BEEEEP BEEEEP. It's that ear-splitting sound a truck makes as it backs up. I jump over to assist, waving the vehicle into place.

"Good morning, Bob!" I call out to the driver.

He gives me a toot-toot blow of the horn and a wave. "Thanks, Carly."

I grab the smoothies off the apple box (film-speak for hollow wooden crates, used for a variety of purposes — kinda like me) and turn toward the set at a half-run disguised as a purposeful walk.

"Carly?"

I turn my sunshine how-can-I-help face around with a big smile. "Yes?"

I lock eyes with someone who makes me gasp involuntarily. Very involuntarily. My heart leaps into my throat, my knees get wobbly, and I think maybe my hair gets frizzier. Because it's Boone, as in Boone my one-high-school-summer boyfriend. The one that broke my sixteen-year-old heart. Because of course he did, with those almost-gold brown eyes of his, which right now are looking deeply into mine.

2

He frowns a little. "Carly? It's me, Boone."

Like a dozen years would keep me from recognizing him. He takes a step in my direction, and I take a step backward. I suddenly remember the smoothies, which I've been holding at the same slightly off angle as my gaping jaw. The beetroot ginger leaked a little.

"Oh, hey. Wow. Huh." You would never know English is my first language.

"Hi," he says softly, slowly. I look back up into his eyes, against my better judgment. "Hi Car," he practically whispers. It's like his entire being goes into slow-mo and soft focus. And that voice from so long ago hits me right in the heart —

What am I doing? I was just a kid last time I saw this guy. I straighten my posture and remember that I am an adult woman who is currently at work on a film in New York City. I try for a bright smile. "What are you doing here?"

"I drove in."

That doesn't really answer my question but it's none of my business anyway. He pushes back his dark blond hair, and I remember how it used to be longer and fall across his eyes when he smiled.

"Drove in from Vermont? Where did you park?"

That may not be the most pressing issue here, but it does make Boone smile.

"I found a place a couple blocks over, on the street."

"You found street parking in Midtown on a Monday morning?"

His grin gets wider. "It's great to see you, Carly."

No. No, no, no. But my heart beats to the rhythm of yes as I find myself smiling back at him. "Well, crazy running into you. Small world coincidence and all that. But I've got to get these drinks to–"

"It's not totally a coincidence, Car."

"What do you mean, Buh–?" I was going to say his name, but it got stuck behind my solar plexus. "Why?"

"I mean, I had to come into New York anyway but I thought I'd just say hi while I was here. Kind of been wondering when was the last time you were at Goodland?"

He means Goodland Farms, my grandmother's orchard, which she left to my me when she passed away two years ago. No, it's been three years now. I haven't been back to Vermont since then, but the orchard had gone to seed long before she died anyway. It hasn't been an operational apple farm for at least a decade.

"It's been a while," I say. Over Boone's shoulder, I see Maria striding toward me, in full boss mode. "I'm sorry but I'm at work," I tell him. "I have to go."

"Of course, I'm sorry. Just wanted to say hi."

Maria is getting closer now and waving. But a thought occurs to me and before Boone leaves and I don't see him again for over another decade, I have to ask: "How did you find me?"

He looks caught, and a little embarrassed. "Instagram," he says.

I let out a laugh at the idea of Boone Akers on social

media. Which maybe didn't even exist the last time we were together.

Boone clears his throat. "I saw that you had been shooting in this neighborhood, and I just looked for all the trucks."

"Carly, where have you been?" Maria rushes up, not at all hesitant to interrupt. "Who is this?" she asks, barely looking at Boone.

Just as I say "Nobody," Boone says "An old friend."

I try to cover. "I just meant, nobody to do with the movie," I say.

But Boone is already backing away and giving us both a friendly nod goodbye. He turns and strides down the street, probably back toward his fairy-tale parking spot that he can't even properly appreciate because he's used to parking effortlessly wherever he wants in a small town. He still walks the same, relaxed and head held high, as if he has all the time in the world. He's probably smiling at people, like a real out-of-towner. And he still wears those faded jeans.

"Carly? Hello! Earth to Carly. Follow me."

Maria is in her forties, with fashionably premature gray hair cut in an expensive bob that bounces with every nervous tic. That's one of Maria's life theories: an expensive haircut is the best money you can spend. I wouldn't know, because all I do to my long dark curls is corral them into scrunchies or banana clips. Today, I'm wearing both but that doesn't stop the frizz from falling around my face.

"Who are those drinks for?" Maria raises an eyebrow but doesn't slow her pace through base camp. "Never mind, I don't want to know. We need to alert all the residents in the building that we'll be shooting until at least seven tonight."

"I already did. And I helped Mr. Sandoval clean his windows."

"His apartment's not in the shot."

"Oh, I know." I see the costumer trying to steam wrinkles out of a hanging dress, so I stop to quickly hold the skirt out for her using my free hand. "But we want all the residents to be happy."

"Carly!" A burst of steam puffs up and clouds Maria's glasses.

"Sorry! Just a sec. This is for the next scene."

The costumer smiles at me but Maria does not. "Carly, you are the assistant *location* manager." Maria is annoyed but affectionate. "Look, I know you mean well. But it's the last week of shooting — I think by now everyone else can handle their own job."

I nod. She's right. And the dress looks perfect.

Maria moves on and I try to keep up. She loud-whispers to me as we speed-walk toward set. "Guess what I heard. A series is coming to town."

Still balancing the drink tray, I slow to move some traffic cones into perfect position. "Really?"

"Twenty-two episodes, which could mean months of work. For both of us." She winks.

Her vote of approval means a lot to me. I give Maria a genuine smile as I push an apple box out of the walking path. It could trip someone there.

"Maria, you know I'd love to be your assistant again. What locations are they looking for this time?"

"It all takes place in a big house in the country-"

But I don't hear the rest because I see the prop guy, who is walking in front of us, drop something. I run ahead to pick up the piece of paper and hand it to him. Realizing what I've done, I turn and rush back to Maria. "You were saying?"

Maria takes a long look at me. She's not smiling, but there's kindness in her eyes. "A couple of years ago, when I first hired you, I thought it might not be a fit. How many women with business degrees want to roll up their sleeves and work on film crews?"

"Oh no, I love to work hard."

"Almost too hard. Carly, you cannot do every job on set."

"I like to make myself useful! Sometimes people can use a little help."

"You can't rescue everyone. You need to focus on your own work."

I nod, trying to toughen up. Maria is trying to help me. "You're right. I will."

"Now please just get on set and make sure nothing happens to the Shawcross' apartment."
I rush toward the house. As I pass the sound mixer, I see

7

he's trying to pull his equipment cart across a cable hump and I offer a helpful shove. He gives me a grateful nod, but I don't turn around to see Maria's reaction. I just keep hurrying toward set.

TWO

The living room set is a found location, meaning the production designer loved it as-is so I negotiated with the homeowner, Ms. Shawcross, to shoot in there without moving out the furniture. The place has a sweet little millennial-grandma vibe: thrift store antiques interspersed with things from Anthropologie. Rupert, the director, is an artist with a capital A, and he'd probably like it if I ended that word with an E as well. His hair is going gray like Maria's, but not prematurely. He's looking into his little monitor video screen, supervising as the cinematographer frames up the two actors. I hang back, waiting for the perfect smoothie delivery moment.

"Good, good. What are we waiting for?" Rupert's British accent rings out. "Let's shoot this, people."

I take a step to the side so I can have a better view, and that's when I see it. A Siberian Husky on the couch. It's an absolutely beautiful animal and I have no idea where it came from. It certainly wasn't in the script.

I step forward, excusing myself to a grip and a makeup artist as I push by. "Wait! Excuse me!" My voice shakes a little.

Rupert doesn't hear me, or doesn't want to. "Are we rolling? People, come on!"

My throat is thoroughly cleared as I take another step forward. "Um, excuse me! The homeowner has allergies and there can be absolutely no dogs in here."

Rupert definitely hears me, along with everyone else in the room, but it doesn't stop the momentum.

"Rolling!" the assistant director announces.

"Speed," the sound mixer affirms.

"A-Camera mark." The camera assistant claps the slate.

"And…" Rupert is about to say *action* —

"I'm sorry! But we can't!"

Rupert snaps his head around toward me, barely veiled annoyance. "What is it?"

Now that I have the floor, I don't want it. "We can't have dogs in here." My voice is higher pitched than usual. "The location contract clearly states that we won't—"

"Then pay the pet deposit, Carly darling. It's your job to keep the location owners happy. It's my job to say what's in the shot." He turns back to the camera. "And…ACTION."

As silently as possible, I slink back through the bored

crew members. The key grip is cleaning his fingernails with a Swiss Army knife. The sound mixer fiddles with knobs on his equipment cart. I am crossing my fingers that this is the only scene they plan to use this Siberian Husky. Where did this giant dog come from, anyway? It's absolutely gorgeous. Maybe it's one of those hypoallergenic breeds. I balance the smoothies and google it — nope, it says Siberian Huskies are known for their thickly furred double coat.

"Cut!" says Rupert.

"Going again!" says the assistant director.

Through the window, I see Ms. Shawcross approaching. She said she had to be at work all day! Homeowners observing shooting is one of my least favorite parts of the job. It's never quite what they expect. What's in front of the camera is a tiny perfect slice of un-reality, but the rest of the room is generally what's described, in technical terms, as a hot mess. A tangle of cables and apple boxes and coffee cups.

I hurry to the door to intercept. "Ms. Shawcross!" I whisper. "They're about to roll again."

"I'll be quiet as a mouse!"

And she breezes past me in her excitement to see the filming. She's all smiles, craning her neck to see our hunky co-star, whom I happen to know she thinks is very handsome. And because it's as obvious as a Siberian Husky on a couch, she spies the dog.

"WHAT is that doing in here?! Carly, I told you,

absolutely no dogs!" She reaches up to her nose, as if already feeling itchy.

"Ms. Shawcross, let me apologize. There's been a misunderstanding."

"How could there be? I was so clear — no dogs."

Rupert turns around, all innocence. "Is there a problem with the dog, Carly?"

The entire crew turns toward me, the grip holding his Swiss Army knife in midair. I realize I'm in an impossible situation. Am I going to throw Rupert under the bus for not listening to me, or take the fall myself and act like I didn't tell him?

I square my shoulders and hold my tray of smoothies a little higher. "Ms. Shawcross, I am so, so sorry."

She waits for something else, but I got nothing. "Well, that's just not acceptable. We went over it in detail." She turns to Rupert. "I have allergies."

Rupert can be quite sweet when he wants to be. "Oh, that must be so difficult." But he doesn't always want to be nice: "Carly, where were you this morning when we were setting up this shot?"

I glance down at the smoothies. "I was helping some people."

"You have to be here, to let me know these things *before* we set up the shot."

He's not wrong. I should have stayed on set. That's actually my, like, job.

"I won't let it happen again." I turn to Ms. Shawcross.

"I should have been here. I put it on the callsheet — no dogs." Rupert glares at me, so I reiterate. "But I should have been here."

"Your attitude is not helpful, Carly." He mocks me, slightly under his breath. *Put it on the callsheet.*

"You're right. I'm sorry."

"I need a working atmosphere that's conducive to my creativity!" he tells me. See above, artiste with an E.

"Okay, I understand." I smile as best I can.

Ms. Shawcross is now a little sorry she caused a fuss. "Oh, it's okay. It's not a big deal."

"It is a big deal!" he assures her. "You're allergic. This is unacceptable. Carly, your services are no longer needed on this film."

A moment of pure shock ricochets around the room. The makeup artist lets out a little *Oooh*. The grip slips his pocketknife away. The two actors exchange a look.

"Goodbye," Rupert tells me.

This moment does not seem rooted in reality. What just happened? Was I just fired? I look around the room but suddenly no one will make eye contact with me. Except Rupert, and I don't want his.

Reeling, I try to gather myself and act with some integrity.

"Ms. Shawcross, my sincere apologies. A complete deep cleaning is included in your contract."

"Oh, I feel just terrible," she says.

"It's fine!" I hand the tray of smoothies to the assistant

director and with as much calm as I can muster, walk out of the room. When I get outside the door, I notice a piece of litter on the ground. I pick it up and throw it in the trashcan. It reminds me of my career.

* * *

Within minutes, I'm handing over my walkie-talkie to Maria. She doesn't want to accept it, but she does.

"He can't fire my assistant!" Then she realizes, "Yes, he can."

I slip off the lanyard with my ID badge and hand that to her as well. "I mean, I wasn't there when they were setting up the shot, so —" I shrug.

"I hate to say it."

"But I need to focus on my own job." Despite feeling incredibly down, I try for optimism. "There's always the next show. Like that upcoming TV series?"

Maria takes a deep breath. "Rupert is also directing that show. That's who told me about it."

I deflate. What have I done?

Maria tries to be nice. "Look, tempers flare, but these things can blow over."

"I hope so. If not, I'm looking for not just a job, but probably someone else to work for. Maria, you're a great boss. Thank you for everything. All the opportunities."

She gives me a big hug and some advice. "Call Rupert in a few days and apologize. He loves to be right, and he loves the drama of the moment." The empathy in her eyes is slowly replaced with something else. "Wait a minute, what am *I* going to do now? I need a new assistant!"

I have to laugh, but it doesn't dissipate the sadness. "I wish I could help."

"That's the problem! Too much doing others' work, not enough taking care of your own." But under her words, Maria's fond smile says volumes.

"If you need anything at all, just call me," I say.

"Go take care of yourself for once. Quit trying to rescue everyone else."

THREE

M y mother lives in a sleek, luxury high-rise and that's appropriate because she's all of those things as well. How did I get to be rumpled and short(ish)? Where her eyes are brown, mine are bright blue, and where her nails are red, mine are chewed. But Mom's building has the nicest doorman ever, Tommy, and he doesn't mind that I'm in Doc Martens instead of Louboutins.

"Welcome, Miss Walton! How you doin' today?"

After a little small talk, I'm on my way up in the high-speed elevator, and already dreading that I have to tell Mom I got fired. I decide to distract myself by seeing if I can find Boone on Instagram, but I don't see him on my followers list. I'm really surprised and also kind of touched that he reached out, or that he even remembered me after our super-short summer fling in North Haven... The elevator dings.

WHAT HAPPENED TO MY EX

I knock lightly, but the door's ajar because of course Tommy buzzed up that I was coming. "Mom? I'm here."

The place is all minimalist furniture and maximalist view. I breathe in the skyline and feel awestruck for the millionth time by all that is New York City.

My mom, Arlene, comes out of the bedroom, little earbuds visible above her sparkling diamond studs as she talks on the phone. "Look, we have two backup offers. Final proposal, take it or leave it." She glances my way and whispers, "Posture."

I stand up straighter. I grab an apple off the kitchen island and walk to the wall of windows, enjoying the expanse of city below. I've always loved heights.

Mom wraps up her call, decisively. "I'll give your investor until eight a.m. tomorrow, then I'm going to the next person on the list." And she clicks off her phone abruptly.

"No goodbye for them?" I ask.

"No hello for me?" she counters, pointing to her cheek.

I walk over to kiss her and she takes away my apple. "Don't eat this. Let's go get sushi tonight. My treat."

"I don't feel like going out to dinner, Mom. I'm sorry."

"You're tired because you're doing grunt work on that film set all day instead of actually producing a movie, like you should. On the next show, you need one of those chairs with your name across the back."

Mom works in finance, but she's very invested in my film career. She thinks I should be running the show instead of running around the set.

"Well, I may not be working on the next project at all."

She gives me a look — *what happened??*

* * *

Half an hour later, I'm sitting at the kitchen island, a bit dejected, as Mom paces.

"Carly! Didn't business school teach you anything about division of labor?"

"I thought helping people was good business."

Her whole manner says tsk, tsk, tsk. "Well, you need to move onto the next project ASAP. And with a promotion this time. You should be producing not working in locations."

How many times has she said this to me over the past couple of years? In my mom's mind, producing films is a business like any other and my degree means I should be in charge of things. She doesn't understand how difficult that is to achieve in the high-stress movie industry.

"Mom, please."

"What? You would be a great producer. Believe in yourself, alright? You have a chance to actually make money and build a real career, not run around getting coffee for people."

"I don't get coffee for people!" I say, neglecting to mention the smoothies. I sigh and rub that little third eye spot in the center of my forehead. "Mom, can we not do this, just for tonight? I was recently fired and I'd like to limit my unhappiness to just that subject, instead of the entirety of my existence and all my life choices."

"I was trying to help," she says, but she gives me a loving look. She and I may be different, but we're still very close. Usually.

"Besides, I might take a week or so off before I even look for another job," I say.

"Hm, okay." She gets a text and is barely listening to me. "Come on." She picks up her purse. "Natsumi's? Let me take you to a nice dinner."

"I was thinking I might go out to Granny's for a while."

Mom puts her purse back down, fully shocked. And by the way, me saying that I might go to Vermont has absolutely nothing to do with any gold-flecked brown eyes or faded blue jeans. Seriously, it doesn't.

"Carly, why? You don't have to go all the way up there just to sell Granny's place."

I'm not sure that's what I meant, but I say, "Can I sell it?"

"Of course!" she says. "Granny's will has been probated. Everything was transferred into your name as the sole heir. And now you just contact some local realtor to handle the sale. Easy."

It's weird that she and I have never discussed this. Somehow, Granny and the orchard and all of Vermont is a sore subject for Mom, so neither one of us ever bring it up. I mean, I don't even use maple syrup in her presence. And now when I actually do bring it up, it's just assumed that I'm selling the place. I mean, of course I probably am selling it…and wait, do I already have a buyer in Boone? Why else would he have looked me up? Wow — the realization that he probably wants to buy the place hits me for the first time.

"I haven't decided if I'm selling the farm yet."

Mom gives me an arched eyebrow. It's not the first one I've gotten in my twenty-eight years on this earth. It's not the first one I've gotten this week.

"At least not right now," I hedge.

"What are you going to do with that tumble-down place?"

I shrug.

She softens a bit. "Granny's been gone for three years. And you've never once set foot on the farm since she died. It's time, Carly."

I hate to admit it, but she makes a good point. "It's sad to go out there," I say.

"See? You'll feel so much better once the place is out of your hair. I never could stand small town living." I've heard this a thousand times before. "I know, Mom."

"All those gossips in your business, talking about everything you do."

"Maybe you were just the most popular girl in town," I tease.

"Shush!" She smiles. "Carly, you do need to take care of this. Get rid of the place. I'll make some calls."

"No, Mom. I'll handle it. I'm going to go up there and take care of it myself."

She gives me a look and I can tell she's wondering whether or not to push me on this.

But I interrupt her thoughts with, "Hey, I actually am hungry for some sushi now."

FOUR

The train is always romantic to me, and I grab a window seat on the left side so I can have that view of the Hudson River as we head upstate. Leaving Manhattan behind, I settle in and enjoy the morning sunlight on the water. I'm not going to think about Boone, which means I'm thinking about Boone just by thinking, "I won't think about Boone." It's a very meta-anxiety moment. Deep breath, let go of any ex-boyfriend energy. He's probably not in North Haven anymore anyway. Vermont's a big place. Said no one, ever.

Boone and I first met at a street dance the summer before I went to eleventh grade. It was the last summer I ever went to stay for weeks with Granny, and it was the first time I had started to find North Haven boring, after years of hearing my mother call it that. But the small town quickly got very unboring that summer when a tall, blond guy in Wranglers walked up and asked me to dance. It was like-at-first-dance, and we spent the next couple of weeks in a whirlwind small town romance. Think ice cream cones from the drug store and second-run movies at the old theater, all of it between kisses and laughing. So. Much. Laughing. Boone was about to leave for college, but he and I didn't talk much about any of that. We clicked in this deep meant-to-be-way, finishing each other's sentences and liking all the same things and oh, the electricity. By the time I left a few weeks later, I thought I'd found my true love forever life partner. Ah youth. He only wrote me one letter, and it got misplaced in the mail somehow — my mom didn't find the envelope until weeks later, and by then I felt like it was too late to write back. The letter had been postmarked in Oregon anyway, and I didn't think he'd want to receive a letter from a high school girl while he was away at college all the way across country. A couple of years later, I remember Granny telling me that Boone's father had died unexpectedly. I told her to pass on my regrets, but I never reached out directly, By then I was in college myself and I only thought of his smile and his laugh and his kisses occasionally.

As the train hits the countryside, I start to relax. The Hudson Valley in springtime is so beautiful. Why do so many human beings cram themselves onto that one little island of Manhattan where we have to build houses on top of each other, dozens of stories high, just to fit in the space? Meanwhile, there are all these empty rolling hills with actual trees and grass and…all that other green stuff. What's the point of cities anyway? Of course that sushi was really, really good last night. I do love New York City, it can just be very hard to, you know, exist.

The last time I was in North Haven for any length of time was when Granny was sick, and the place had looked anything but beautiful to me then. Mom and I had made this same journey, but it had been full of sadness and anxiety. Come to think of it, every trip Mom and I ever made here had some unspoken tension between Granny and Mom. When I was growing up, I'd been dropped off in the summers to stay with Gran by myself though — whenever Mom had a business trip. Business trip being code for new boyfriend, obviously. I didn't mind. The last thing I wanted to do was meet Mom's latest beau, especially since they never lasted.

We pull into the train station and I grab my little suitcase off the rack. With my adult eyes, I can see North Haven is a picturesque and welcoming small town. It used to feel like freedom and maybe it still does, a bit. I get off the train and walk down Main Street, passing a coffee shop called Cake My Day that's bustling. I stop in for a coffee with heavy cream, and I remember I haven't eaten since I left my apartment hours ago. I add an almond croissant to my order, because I can pretend the "almond" has some protein in it and I'm eating a decent breakfast. The croissant is way beyond decent, I realize — protein or no, something this tasty has got to be good for me on some level.

I sip my coffee and eat my croissant as I walk Main Street, re-acclimating myself to the town. There's the radio station — it's still here! North Haven's public KTRE. I cross the street and peer inside and sure enough, the studio is still visible, where you can see whatever radio announcer is currently live at work. It's a young woman about my age, and I recognize her. It's Celia, a girl I used to be friends with a little bit in the summers. I'm sure she'd never recognize me though. She speaks into the mic, animated — and I can hear her voice through the exterior speakers that broadcast outside so everyone who walks by can hear the station. She talks about things like a fundraiser for North Haven Pets Alive, about Vermont's famous local novelist Archer Mendez's latest book release, and an upcoming Apple Blossom Festival.

I smile and walk on. It's relaxing here. I guess I'll call an Uber soon and head out to Granny's. I'm assuming her old pick-up truck is still there, and I'll be able to drive that. Of course, it will certainly need a charging up — what's that called? Jumping start?

"You came."

I don't have to spin around to know that's Boone's voice. Gulp. I guess I knew I *might* run into him, but not within minutes of arriving with a mouth full of pastry. I swallow and push back my curls and stand up straight (with Mom's voice saying, 'Posture!' in my head).

I turn toward him, feigning nonchalance but "Oh, hey, Boone" comes out full of chalance, unfortunately.

His Carhartt jacket is the color of his eyes. If that doesn't sound cute, think of a lion with flecks of gold embedded in light brown irises, staring at you... Is he hungry or is he bored? Impossible to tell.

Boone finally clears his throat. "I'm surprised to see you. I didn't think you'd ever actually come."

What is that supposed to mean? "Well, I'm here."

"And you're going to the farm."

I don't know if that's a global observation or just small talk. "Yeah, I'm about to call an Uber, and go out there."

I detect a smile at the word Uber, but I don't care.

Boone says, "I'm not sure what Arnie's doing."

"Arnie?"

"North Haven's only Uber driver. He might be watching *The Bold and the Beautiful* right now. He never misses his show."

I nod, fully aware I'm being made fun of. "I'm not in a hurry."

"Tell you what," says Boone. "I could take you."

I'm about to say absolutely not, but I've done enough inner work to know not to reject a perfectly good ride when the universe offers one. Especially if that ride might include jumper cables. (That's what they're called! My subconscious came up with it.)

"Okay, sure."

"I just have to drop something off first." He gingerly pulls open his jacket and I see what he's been holding under there: a tiny kitten.

26

WHAT HAPPENED TO MY EX

I don't want my knees to go weak, but they do. Because kitten + strapping guy = weak knees. A universal truth. Go ahead and test that out if you want, I stand by it.

"Who is this?" I coo, taking an involuntary step toward him.

"It's a stray. I'm going to take her to the vet's office."

He opens his jacket a little more and moves closer. I reach out and touch the kitten's head with my fingertip, that's how tiny she is. A little orange-and-white striped tabby, she starts purring under my touch.

"Purring, that's a good sign," says Boone.

Something starts purring inside of me too, I think. Boone is tall where I'm not, blond where I'm dark, still where I'm jumpy. He smells like a bonfire last night mixed with a hot shower this morning. It's vaguely familiar and brings back something I found irresistible when I was a dumb teenager.

Good thing I'm a dumb adult now.

"Come on," he says.

Boone walks with purpose down Main Street, and after an undecided two-and-a-half seconds, I follow along.

* * *

The vet's office is bustling. How many small town Vermont locals have sick pets? Apparently quite a few on this beautiful spring day. Boone walks right up to the desk, where a woman in her seventies with bright purple eyeglasses types into a computer.

27

"Hey, Irene."

"Hey, Boone." She looks over the top of her glasses. "Here we go again. What is it this time?"

Boone smiles and holds up the kitten. "She was out by the trashcans behind Belichek's. All alone. She's got a little cut on her leg. Looks like it might be infected."

"Doc's all booked up."

"Not surprised. Feels like every month you get busier. This place is bursting at the seams."

The kitten mews. Boone gives Irene a pleading look, with a charming smile thrown in for good measure.

Irene turns to me, "What are we going to do with this guy?" She shakes her head and gives in. "Okay, Boone, you're practically as much a vet as Doc Mullins is by now, whether you ever finished veterinary school or not."

At that Boone seems to stop smiling.

Irene reaches out and pets the kitten. "I'm sure Doc won't mind if you use the back room."

"Thanks, Irene."

Boone heads back, and once again I follow.

FIVE

After Boone fixes up the kitten's cut with some ointment and gauze, he gives her wet kitten chow and leaves her in a cozy crate in the vet's back room, until he can find her a home. We head out toward the farm in Boone's truck, and I'm so curious about him that I'm actually inspecting the trash on the floorboard. A coffee cup from Cake My Day and bits of straw — or is that hay? Is there a difference?

On the edge of town, we pass the roadside stand with strawberries which looks exactly the same as the one I used to stop at with Granny. She'd make strawberry shortcake with Sara Lee poundcake and frozen Cool Whip. Hey, I never said she was a great cook — but boy, did I love that dessert.

The radio is playing so we don't have to talk, and Boone rolls down both the windows. Somehow, him rolling down the passenger window for me without asking puts me in an edgy down-with-the-patriarchy mood, but I tell myself to get a grip and just enjoy that spring breeze blowing my curls around. Boone reaches to turn up the radio and it's probably just a coincidence that it's a song which was popular during our summer fling. A fellow Carly, Carly Rae Jepsen, tells someone to "Call Me Maybe." That irresistibly catchy pop tune lifts my heart and spins it around, and I'm remembering listening to it in a very similar truck, on these same roads, with this same guy. Was that a thing, or am I dreaming it? Either way, the bouncy music has me not worrying about anything but this moment. It's a beautiful day in Vermont orchard country. And is that Boone's knee bouncing in rhythm? I avert my eyes, trying not to care if he remembers us listening to this song or not.

"Remember this?" he says, right on cue. But he's not talking about the song. "We saw that family who ran out of gas right there?"

I do remember now – it was a minivan with a mom and dad and a couple of kids. "Oh yeah!"

Boone continues, "We were on our way to the movies to see the latest Batman, but you made me stop. You just had to help."

"Well, of course. That's the neighborly way around here, right?"

"That's right. You fit right in. That's why I always thought you might wind up in North Haven."

30

There's a beat of awkward silence. "Can I ask you something, Boone?"

"Sure."

"Did Batman catch the Joker? I never found out."

He laughs as he turns off the country highway, onto Granny's little dirt road leading to the orchard. A gate with an arch above it is marked Goodland Farm, and it brings back memories — I used to think it was so amazing and grand, but now there's rust and it's slightly askew. I'll have to fix that, after I get a ladder. And some tools. And figure out how to use them.

Yeah, I'd better go ahead and sell this place. We just pulled in and I'm already feeling overwhelmed.

"I can't believe we're here," I say — partly just to make conversation.

Boone gives me a sideways grin, and I think he's about to go down memory lane with me. The old days, me and him…

"You can't believe it, even though we've been in a truck heading here for fifteen minutes? But somehow it takes you by surprise?"

"Shut up," I say, holding on for dear life as he goes way too fast on the deeply-rutted dirt road.

Boone chuckles and lets up on the gas. "When was the last time you were here?"

My joking mood evaporates. I shrug and push back my curls like I do a lot when I'm nervous. I guess I just like the fruitlessness of pushing them off my face and having them spring right back in front of my eyes.

"Oh, you know…" I mutter out the window.

"You mean, not since…?"

"The funeral."

Boone lets out a big sigh. "I didn't think so," he says. There's more disapproval than empathy in his voice, or maybe I'm just imagining that.

The farm road doesn't go by any of the orchards, it just cuts across a pasture and up over a big hill. As we crest it, I hold my breath — and there she is. Granny's house.

It's an old timber farmhouse. The place is past its prime, sure — but still inviting, with its deep shady porches and rough-hewn log columns and weathered metal roof. I let out my breath, overcome with emotion at the sight of this place. All of a sudden I'm a little girl again, and my mom's dropping me off for a summer vacation and I can almost taste the pure freedom. Climbing trees and swimming and making ice cream on the back porch. In the evenings, I'd go through Granny's button box, full of treasures. And I'd make up imaginary board games where thieves came to steal apples at Goodland Farms and brave grandmothers fought off the hordes. Granny was my safe place, that's for sure.

And this is the first time I've been back since the funeral.

Boone parks and throws open his door, jumping out and heading toward the house. I'm not sure if he realizes I just got a little emotional and wants to get as far away from me as possible, or if he's completely oblivious. Before I get out, I flip down the sun visor and glance in the little rectangular mirror. My blue eyes are a little misty, and my cheeks look too pink. I put my crazy curls back in a clip, and apply some peppermint chapstick that I have in my jeans pocket. I just want to feel ready to face —

KNOCK, KNOCK on the passenger window makes me jump.

"Are you putting on *makeup* right now?" Boone peers through the glass at me, bemused.

I point to my ears and silently mouth the words, "I can't hear you."

His wry grin and shake of the head make me want to smile back at him, but I resist. I open the truck door and hop down. "Sorry to keep you waiting."

"No problem, it's only been three years." Boone tips his gimme-cap from North Haven Vet Hospital.

"More like a dozen." I immediately regret saying that.

We meet eyes... I'm the first to look away. I turn toward the farmhouse.

He points the way with one hand, as the fingers of his other hand graze my lower back, ever so lightly. It's a tiny gesture of politeness or an outrageously flirtatious come-on, you be the judge. Just kidding, I know it's nothing — so why are my nerve endings all on high alert? Being close to Boone is bringing back feelings that I haven't let myself feel for — well, for at least since we were just in the truck two minutes ago.

How does he do this to me?! Just a silly boy, I tell myself.

I am a grown woman, and I am here to inspect a property that I own. I throw my shoulders back and stride toward the farmhouse confidently, all business. And I trip over a stone, even though I'm in sneakers. That's what I get for holding my head too high. Can't see the ground. I hear Boone snicker, but I don't turn around.

I'm almost all to the porch when he says, "Carly, watch out!"

I stop in my tracks. A bear? A snake? An axe murderer?

"That's poison ivy," he tells me, moving closer.

"Oh. Thanks."

"I didn't want you to make a rash decision." He smiles at me, all innocent, as if he didn't just make one of the worst jokes available in that moment.

"Dad humor alert," I say.

"More like ivy league humor."

I search my brain for a retort. "That's joke's as painful…as poison ivy."

"There's no pun there," he tells me.

"Okay, you win."

"*Leaf* it to me," he says.

At that point, I have to actually laugh. I give the poison ivy a wide berth, and walk onto the porch stairs. The third step's old wooden board squeaks under my foot in a way that brings back a thousand memories.

"I spent summers here my whole life," I say. "Some of my earliest memories are on this porch. There used to be a swing—"

"It's in the barn. It fell down. Needs new ropes."

I wonder for a second how he knows where the old porch swing is, but I let it go. He obviously wants to buy the place and has probably been out here poking around. And why not, since it will probably be his soon.

"Look at this," Boone says. He's peering up into the eave. "A bird's nest."

I go up on tiptoes, but still can't quite see. "I need a ladder," I say — but turns out I actually don't need one because at that moment, Boone puts his hands on my waist and gives me a boost up. The little perfect birds' nest with its delicate eggs is clearly visible, a thing of beauty. "Wow," I say. But I'm thinking just as much about the way he's holding me against him as the beautiful little nest.

"Mama's probably around here somewhere watching us." He drops me back down, as if lifting me up was nothing.

I try to get back to business. "You know, Goodland Farm is 200 acres," I say.

"Two hundred and sixteen," he replies, not taking his eyes off me.

"And this house is quite old," I tell him. "Historic even. Built by settlers over a hundred years ago."

"In 1872," he says, reaching up to touch the wall. "By German immigrants. It's tongue and groove woodwork, with these old-growth timber beams. All hewn by hand."

"I can see you've done your research already."

"Research on the farm? Never thought of it quite like that."

35

I sigh. So he's going to play hard to get, like a dumb country boy? Well, I'm not going to be cheated out of what this place is worth.

"Do you at least have comps?" I ask in my most business-y tone. "A listing price for an intact parcel as big as this, even without the orchards, has to be considerable." I'm particularly proud of the phrase "intact parcel" and I half smile, waiting for him to respond.

Boone kicks an imaginary rock off the porch, deep in thought. Finally, he takes a deep breath and does not smile as he looks at me. "Are you telling me you're *selling* your own grandmother's farm, Ms. Carly Walton?"

The disgust on his face is suddenly loud and clear. I feel my heartbeat rising. I've misread this situation completely.

"So you don't want to buy it." I attempt a joke: "Or if you do, you might want to rethink your negotiating."

But Boone doesn't laugh. "No, I'm not here to buy the place. I'm just a caretaker, who worked for your grandmother toward the end when she couldn't do everything around here by herself anymore. And after she passed, I kept coming around, checking on the place."

"I didn't realize she ever hired someone."

"She never paid me. Not in cash. But your granny let me board my horses in exchange for helping her out." He doesn't appear to be getting less mad. "I think she trying to keep the place in good shape for her beloved granddaughter."

"Oh!" I literally cringe at those sharp words.

He just shrugs in reply. "Just being truthful."

This is ridiculous. I don't want to fight with Boone Akers. I mean, there are worse things than hanging out with your ex. Like a root canal without novocaine. "Look, I'm sorry. Why did you come find me in New York, if you don't want to buy the place?"

He starts to say something, then stops himself with great effort. He shakes his head gruffly — he's not going to answer that question.

"Okay, Boone. I'm sorry for the misunderstanding," I say, feeling confused and idiotic.

"So I don't have any *comps* for you, Carly. I can't tell you what this place is worth." His gaze makes me squirm. "Any more than I can tell you what the sky is worth. What is the sound of the wind blowing through the trees worth?"

"Okay, let's not be dramatic."

"What is the home of your own grandmother worth?" He holds my gaze, as if challenging me.

"Okay, that's enough. You don't know anything about my situation, about my career."

"I know that a family legacy homestead is meaningless to some people who would rather drift from movie to movie working, instead of putting down roots."

"Stop it." He's getting under my skin now.

"You're right, it's none of my business." He does seem genuinely sorry all of a sudden.

I can't decide whether to be highly insulted by the way

he's judging me or slightly gratified that he knows all the movies I've been working on. "Boone, I'm sorry if I misunderstood. And it's not that I don't have good memories here, but yes -- I have a career back in Manhattan. So sue me. We can't all live out in the country and be — whatever you are."

"Happy. That's what I am." He heads for his truck. "Let's go," he orders.

"I'm staying here."

His shoulders sag in irritation. "You want to stay out here, by yourself?"

I nod, too proud to reconsider. "I'll be fine."

A long beat, then he gets in his truck and turns the key. I hate leaving it this way between us, especially since he's been helping out Granny — and I guess me — for so long.

I rush up to the truck before he pulls away. He rolls down his window.

"Boone?" He waits for me to figure out what to say. "Thank you for taking care of this place. For Granny."

He looks out over the old, overgrown orchards. "She used to tell me again and again, 'Oh Carly, she loves this place. It's in her heart.'"

I swallow back some threatening tears. Boone throws it in gear and drives away. I watch as the dust is kicked up behind his truck on the rutted road that leads out of the farm.

SIX

My sadness turns to indignation pretty darn quickly. Who does that guy think he is? What does he care if I sell the place? I'm so agitated that I call up a local realtor and tell her to come out as soon as she can, which turns out to be immediately. I can sell this place if I want to, and I have a career and I live in New York City. Who is Boone, but some local guy with brown eyes that have flecks of gold in them who carries around baby kittens and—

I'm glad when the realtor shows up. Her name is Crystal and she doesn't hate the idea of selling, not one little bit. Her appraising eye takes in the place. "This house is quaint! A mess, but quaint."

"It needs some work, sure. But this farmhouse was built in 1872 by German immigrants. These old growth timber beams were all hewn by hand." I glance up at the birds' nest as the mama settles over her eggs. "You think there are some interested buyers out there for a place like this?"

Crystal sighs. "I'll be honest. The only one I know of is this big developer, Silp-Co. But even that's not a sure thing. They'll have a *lot* of questions about this place."

"Well, let's see if we can answer them. I need to sell it and get back to Manhattan."

Before Crystal leaves, she tells me the first order of business is to make sure the title to the farms has been officially transferred into my name at the county courthouse.

Granny's truck is stored out in the barn, right next to where the old porch swing is stored. All the stalls are clean, and so is the pasture that's attached, where three horses mill about. They must be Boone's and that's why he's been out here so much. They're beautiful, sweet animals and they come to say hello but grow bored when I don't have any treats in my pockets.

The truck starts right up, and I figure I must have Boone to thank for that. The old-timey pickup is the kind with wooden slats down the sides, and it has GOODLAND FARM hand-painted on the door, faded now. Granny used to park this truck at the farmer's markets in the summer and sell fresh apples right out of the back. When I was little, she'd let me be the cashier — but half the time, she wouldn't charge people full price anyway. She usually bargained with people for them to pay even less. It's a sweet memory that makes my throat tighten. It's funny how these feelings are coming back while I'm here. All the more reason to get rid of this place and avoid the sadness.

Coming into North Haven from this direction, I'm struck by what a quintessential little Vermont town it is, with its church spires and Colonial homes and red brick mills along the river that winds through town. I'm not sure I properly appreciated all the beauty when I was a kid.

When I park in front of the courthouse, I pull out my phone, quickly dialing before I lose my nerve. The recorded message, in Rupert's British accent comes on: *Hello. You know what to do, darling.*

Okay, here I go. "Hi, Rupert? This is Carly Walton. The location assistant. Obviously. I hope the last week of shooting went well. After I left." I cringe — why did I bring that up? "Anyway, I'm sorry if I was disruptive in any way. I just wanted to say that I heard you might be doing another project. And I'd love to be — to be involved. So, thank you and -- " Wrap it up, Carly! "So. Bye. Take care."

I click off the call. "Well, that was incredibly awkward," I say aloud to myself.

I walk through town, surprised at the bit of hustle bustle in this little place. I step into Belichek's General Store, which looks like the best option for some supplies.

"Miss Carly Walton," says a white-haired little man who must be in his eighties.

"Hello?" I smile, although I am a little freaked out to be name-checked like this.

He nods and shakes his head, his smile widening. "I

don't expect you to remember me, but I've seen plenty of photos of you. I was a good friend of your Granny's the last few years of her life. She liked to keep it quiet but," he winks. "A real good friend! I'm Huey Belichek."

"Nice to see you, Mr. Belichek."

"Me and your granny, we had some fireworks together."

"Is that so?"

"Huge explosions. Knock your socks off!"

Okaaay. What am I supposed to say to that?

Mr. Belichek points to sparklers and bottle rockets on the shelves. "Your grandmother loved fireworks towards the end. Even when it wasn't Fourth of July, she'd say, any night was a good night for a celebration, as far as she was concerned. Oh, she kept me young."

He is lost in a moment's reverie. I look around the old-fashioned store, which is jam-packed with a little bit of everything.

"You know, I do remember — when I spent summers with her, she used to bring me to this shop. On Saturdays, I think. We'd get some kind of root beer candy…"

"Root beer barrels!" He shows me where a big glass jar of root beer-flavored hard candies sits, at the end of the counter.

"Yes!" It gives me all the feels to see it. "You still have them."

"I'd never get rid of these. They were your grandmother's favorite." He reaches inside with a pair of silver tongs and drops a candy in the palm of my hand.

I tear off the cellophane wrapper and the candy is sweet on my tongue. It takes me right back to childhood. "Thanks, Mr Belichek."

"She loved you so much, Carly. I'm glad you've come back, to keep her memory alive. She always wanted you to have that farm."

Tears spring to my eyes before I have a chance to stop them.

"Now, now," he says. "Even if it took you awhile, you're here today. That's what's important." Suddenly there's a minor ruckus outside. We both turn to look through the store's front window, where a dalmatian is yelping loudly.

Turns out the dog is named Rex and his caretaker is a guy named Whit who's in his thirties and wears a North Haven Fire Department shirt.

"Hey boy, it's okay," he tries to comfort Rex, who is pulling on his leash and moaning. I see the dalmatian has a NHFD collar, so it must be the fire station dog.

A few townspeople have gathered, concerned but keeping their distance from the agitated animal. Mr. Belichek and I look on as Whit holds tightly to Rex's leash -- and who comes hurrying up into the middle of the fray, but Boone. This really is a small town. Geez.

He goes straight to Rex, kneeling in front of the panicked dog.

"Hey, fella, easy," Boone whispers. His calm demeanor quiets everyone's nerves, not just the dog's.

Whit's glad to see Boone. "A bee was buzzing around and I think Rex tried to bite it."

Boone keeps speaking directly to the dog. "Bees don't taste too good, do they? Let me take a look there."

As Boone slowly reaches toward the dog, I find myself speaking out: "You aren't going to reach into that dog's mouth, are you? He's in pain — he could bite you, Boone."

Boone gives me a look that's not anger, but surprise. I'm surprised too — why am I inserting myself into this situation? I guess while I'm in a small town, I might as well be as nosy as everyone else. "Just trying to help," I say.

Whit says, "Maybe I should take him over to the vet."

Rex whines a little, and Boone pets him gently. "Sure, but Doc Mullins is awfully busy. You might be waiting awhile."

Boone looks up at Whit, who nods his assent. Calmly confident, Boone reassures Rex with pats and little sounds as he examines him. Finally he gets to his mouth, and I'm amazed that the dog lets him reach in and look around.

"Hey there boy, you're okay," Boone says. "Mr. Belichek, you have some baking soda in the store, don't you?"

"Yes, sir!"

Boone addresses Whit. "Looks like he was stung alright. It's already swelling. What we're going to do is make a paste out of the baking soda with a little water and rub it right on this spot. It'll bring him some relief."

Rex the dalmatian has already calmed considerably. Whit says, "That would be great."

Boone smiles. "I think he was more shocked than hurt."

I follow Mr. Belichek into the store. "Can I help you?"

"Right up there." He points to a shelf in the grocery section that has baking soda. "And I'll get a container."

As I reach up high for the little orange box, I make conversation. "Boone sure has a way with that dog."

"Oh, he's always loved animals. And more importantly, they love him. That says a lot about a person."

I hand over the baking soda and Mr. Belichek spoons some out, adding a bit of water.

"Maybe he should be a vet," I say.

"He does assist down at Doc Mullins' office sometimes, as a volunteer. He went to vet school for awhile, but it wasn't for him. He's all about natural cures. But Boone's pretty in demand as a farm foreman around here. Pretty much everybody in the county hires him or wants to. He has a way with animals, and he understands the land. Here you go." He hands me the baking soda paste and gives me a wink. "You could do a whole lot worse than Boone Akers."

"What? Oh no! I'm not interested in him as a — like that. I'm just, I was asking because — I mean, he's been working at the farm." I can't believe how flustered I am all of a sudden. Guess this place is making me feel sixteen again in more ways than one.

"Ask Boone how to make your Granny's farm work for you. As a business. He could maybe help."

45

I'm not sure what to say to that, so I hold up the paste. "I better go ahead and take this out."

"Good idea," Mr. Belichek says with a twinkle.

Back out on the street, the dog is calm and the small crowd has dispersed. I kneel next to Boone, holding the bowl of baking soda.

"Thanks," Boone says, all concentration. However upset he was with me earlier, that's all temporarily forgotten because he's so concerned with the welfare of this whimpering dog. "Can you hold Rex's leash?"

"Sure, okay," I say. I'm nervous, but Boone is in calm control. Before I know it, Rex has lain down sweetly, enjoying the soothing paste on his bee sting.

"That's amazing," I say.

"Animals are just like any other person."

I smile at that.

"Well, it's true," says Boone.

"I guess we do all want the same things."

Boone puts a little more paste on Rex's sting. "Oh yeah, like what do you want?"

I think about that carefully. "A job on another movie is what I really need right now."

"I said want, not need."

"Well, I need the job because I *want* security."

"For me, security is having a home." He turns to me. We're kneeling side by side, and our faces are quite close. It's just a passing moment, but I feel the whisper of days past. A memory of what his mouth felt like on mine, all those years ago.

46

"You've got a little baking soda —" Boone reaches up and touches my cheek.

"I put it there on purpose."

We both smile.

Whit walks up. "Okay, I pulled my truck up. Should I load Rex in?"

I jump up, as if caught at something. "Rex is great! I mean, better. What a good dog." I'm aware that I'm speaking a little too loudly.

Boone smiles. "Just put a new paste on that spot every couple of hours, until the pain and swelling subside. If you notice anything else, take him to Doc's right away. But I think Rex is going to be just fine."

The dog leans up against Boone, nudging his thanks.

SEVEN

Boone is loading supplies into the back of his truck as I watch.

"Lemme help!" I say.

"I got it."

"Are you positive? Let me —"

But he loads the last couple of bags into the bed of his truck by himself, and then turns to me. "You sure like to help."

I hate that he already has me tagged and that it rings a bit true. He leans against his truck and smiles. He's that type of relaxed sexy guy who is just comfortable in his own skin. And for some reason, it makes me feel so uncomfortable. He should be uptight like the rest of us.

"So you find a buyer yet?" he asks, teasing in his voice.

"Actually yes. Maybe a company called Silp-Co."

"The developers?!" He's not teasing anymore.

I wanted to get a rise out of him, and I did. "That's right."

"They'll just make it into a cookie-cutter neighborhood."

"I love cookies."

"The Silp-Co brothers are -- "

"Sounds like a boy band from Canada."

"Don't be flip. I can't think of a worse potential buyer."

"Then the question is, can you think of a better one?"

We hold our gaze for a moment, and I feel defiant. I don't need his approval to sell a farm that my grandmother left to me! But when Boone turns away, he looks more sad than disgusted.

"Look, it's not a done deal," I backpedal. "Maybe we'll find someone else? I'm just exploring my options."

"You have nowhere to go but up. Silp-Co's about as bad as they come." He shakes his head. "I mean seriously, Carly."

I bristle at his judgmental tone. "Alright, thanks for the tip, Mr. High and Mighty. If you'll excuse me, I have to go to the County Commissioner's Property Office now."

I walk over to Granny's truck, which I guess is my truck now.

"You mean the commissioner's office at the county courthouse?"

"That's right! I need to go get a clean title so I can sell

49

POPPY CARTER

the farm." I feel like adding *So there!* but I don't.

"You mean the courthouse that's right behind you? The large building in the center of the North Haven town square, that's the tallest thing for miles?"

I know I'm beat, but I try to act unbothered. "Yes, that courthouse." I slam the truck door.

He smiles and I try not to.

As Boone walks away, he says, "I'll be out to take care of my horses in the morning. And I'll be finding another place to board them."

"You don't have to take them yet."

"Sounds like I do. I'll be finding a place as soon as I can."

* * *

The county tax assessor office is on the second floor. I stand at the old-fashioned marble counter while a nice but disorganized middle-aged woman named Samantha searches through some county records.

"I know that title should be right here. Walton, Walton…"

"Can I help you look?"

Samantha opens a different filing cabinet. "Oh, that's okay, honey." She turns to me with a conspiratorial smile. "You know, I went to high school with your mama. I was a cheerleader with her in fact!"

"A cheerleader? My mother? I don't think so."

"Arlene? She sure was."

This throws me for a loop. "My mother was a cheerleader in North Haven?"

"The head cheerleader, as the matter of fact. Kept us all in line."

"That part does sound familiar." We exchange a smile.

Samantha turns to another file drawer. "She never mentioned it?"

I think about it. "No. But I guess she doesn't talk too much about the old days. Always looking forward."

"Well, sometimes it's nice to get in touch with your roots."

Just then a meek fifty-something man comes in.

"Oh, hey Donny," Samantha says matter-of-factly, barely looking up.

Donny is tongue-tied and blushing. "Hi, Samantha. Can I, uh, put up a poster for the Apple Blossom Festival?"

It seems like Donny has a crush on Samantha, but she's oblivious as she searches the files.

"Oh Donny, everyone knows about the festival already, but sure. Go ahead." She's kindly dismissive.

I walk to Donny. "Well, I don't know about it. What's the Apple Blossom Festival?"

Shy Donny hands me a poster about the annual street dance on the town square that's happening next Saturday night. I hold it up to the wall, helping out while he tapes it up.

"I'll bet you're a good dancer, Donny." I smile at him.

"I don't know about that," he says, embarrassed.

"Samantha, do you like to dance?" I say.

Donny's cheeks redden.

"I found it!" says Samantha, pulling a sheaf of papers from her old metal filing cabinet.

I wave goodbye to Donny as I go to look at the property records. Samantha is happy about finding the paperwork, but her smile suddenly disappears.

"What is it?"

She flips through the pages. "Looks like the taxes haven't been paid in three years, honey. The county is about to foreclose on your property."

She hands me the papers. This can't be right.

"What do you mean, foreclose?" I say.

Her tone is gentle, apologetic. "It looks like, if the taxes aren't paid by the end of this month, they'll auction it off right out from under you."

I take in this shocking news. Wait, I'm sure I'm misunderstanding. "So what happens then? The farm is sold, and the government gets all the profit?"

"Yes...and no. Even when it's auctioned off, you'd still owe the rest of the back taxes."

EIGHT

The extra bedroom in the farmhouse is pretty much just like it was when I always stayed here, once I take off all the sheets draped over the furniture to keep it clean. I dust everything anyway and I run the sheets through the washer and dryer, then make up the bed. I slide under the old quilt and it keeps me warm against the spring night's coolness, with the soft mattress enveloping me. Still, sleep evades me because I know I am about to lose the farm. It's one thing to sell it, but it's another to have it taken away from you. I feel like I am letting Granny down.

I toss and turn fitfully, finally getting up not long before dawn. At a relatively decent hour, I text Boone, asking him to stop by when he comes to feed his horses. I pull on some old jeans and a T-shirt with a flannel for warmth. At least my clothing choices fit in around here, even if I don't. I stand on the back porch and watch how the light of the sunrise hits the dew-covered hills. I can see some spring wildflowers that weren't here even yesterday. Purple asters and yellow goldenrod dot the hills. There are even great angelicas, which are spherical bursts of tiny white flowers. Granny used to say they looked like firecrackers exploding. I didn't know she liked fireworks so much. That must've been after I quit coming around as often.

I climb up on a rocking chair (this is dangerous, kids don't try it at home) and peek at the birds' nest. Three tiny delicate eggs are still there, beautiful and perfectly speckled.

I check my emails and my phone messages and my texts and my everything, but it's very clear there have been no replies from Rupert. The boiling kettle whistles and I make myself a cup of coffee by pouring the hot water into an old speckled enamel pot, over the organic beans I got in town. I couldn't find any sort of coffee filters or coffee grinder, so I crushed the beans with a hammer and threw them straight into the pot. I'm hoping this will work. I drink some out of a heavy diner cup that has a chipped bottom. The coffee is not great, but it is a source of caffeine, so I'll take it. For the first time, I take a good look around Granny's kitchen. Or as I should think of it, my kitchen. At least for the next couple of weeks.

I notice a crumpled child's drawing on yellowed paper, taped to the refrigerator. The fridge is mostly covered with to-go menus and invitations to local events, but I move some magnets for a better look. It's a stick drawing of an adult and a child, labeled "Granny" and "Carly," and a stick horse called "Sassy." I pull down the drawing and smooth it out, almost remembering the exact day I drew this.

"Hello?" calls Boone as he opens the front door.

"Oh, good morning. Come in."

He looks as handsome as ever, freshly showered and in a white T-shirt and jeans. I shoo the butterflies in my stomach.

"Would you like some coffee?"

"Coffee? It's almost time for lunch."

"Very funny."

"I guess one cup won't hurt."

I pour it. "You take it black?"

"So just because I'm a farmhand, I can't like cream and sugar? Talk about preconceived notions."

"Sorry, let me get-"

"I do like it black. I just don't like you assuming I'm not a cappuccino frappe lover these days."

I laugh. "Okay, no preconceived notions. Listen, thanks for coming."

He sips the coffee, noticing the crudely-drawn Granny & Carly & Sassy picture. "So you're an artist now?"

He's making me smile more than I mean to. "Oh yes. One of my many talents."

He takes another sip of coffee and wrinkles his nose. "Along with barista?"

"Hey, I did the best I could. You think you can do better?"

"That would be a hard yes."

We're both smiling, and I'm glad I asked him to stop by today. "Boone, can we start over? We got off on the wrong foot. You got to know my grandmother in recent years, and I think you have an idea of what she'd want. And I need some real advice. Because I've found out some stuff that changes everything."

A beat as he considers me, and then he nods. "Walk with me to the paddock?"

I follow him out the door and across the farm, talking about Crystal the realtor and Samantha at the county office. By the time he is exercising a horse in the round pen, I'm perched on the fence finishing my monologue about back taxes.

"And apparently we don't have much time." My voice is urgent. "The end of the month is just a couple of weeks away. And then the county will foreclose on the farm and just take it from me. I don't know how I let this happen. I should've been more responsible!" I find myself getting emotional.

"Well, you certainly didn't mean for it to happen."

"Not only that, but even if it's auctioned off, I'll still owe the back taxes."

This stops Boone short. "You won't have the farm anymore, *and* you'll still owe money?"

"That's right. I'll be going into debt, deeply into debt. Unless I can get top dollar for the place."

"I guess Silp-Co really is the only option."

"And I don't have much time."

A long moment as Boone considers. He starts exercising his horse again, leading her in a circle around the pen. "I know your grandmother wouldn't want you to go into debt because of her."

"But in order to sell, we'd have to fix things up quickly."

"I'm not familiar with that word — 'we'?"

Through a smile, I make my plea. "Goodland Farms hasn't been cleaned or repaired in so long. It could use some fresh flowers, window washing — well, everything, probably. Do you think you could help me?"

Boone narrows his eyes at me. "Carly, listen…" He hesitates, then continues, choosing his words carefully. "You have to understand, Silp-Co would just be buying this place for the land. There's no need to fix up your granny's house. As much as it pains me, they'll probably tear down that old house right away."

As soon as I hear him say that, I know it's true. "Oh, of course. They don't care about flowerbeds and clean windows, do they."

The silence is heavy until Boone breaks it. "But you know what would be good? If the roads could be repaired a little, so Silp-Co can get to the top of Mount Baldy and see the views. Some people say you can see all the way to Massachusetts on a clear day. I'll call and see if we can get a load of gravel delivered today."

My phone rings and I glance down at it as Boone tells me he knows a guy at the gravel place who can probably help us out. I do a doubletake. "Oh my gosh!" I say.

"What?"

I hop down off the fence, composing myself. "It's a 310 number."

"Friend of yours?"

"Area code 310!"

"Okay."

"That's LA! It's probably a film production. About a job for me."

I throw my shoulders back and try to collect my thoughts. I answer in my professional voice, "Carly Walton."

Clearly audible on the other end of the line: *We've been trying to reach you regarding your car's extended warranty—*

My shoulders sag at the recorded voice and Boone does not suppress his laughter.

NINE

By that afternoon, I'm already behind the wheel of a big rental truck filled with gravel. It's parked on the side of a large hill in the middle of the farm.

Boone calls from behind me, "Okay, take her up, nice and slow!"

He stands down the hill from the truck, motioning me ahead. I put the truck in drive so I can ease up the hill. I stomp on the clutch and yank the gear stick. A horrible grinding noise makes us both cringe.

"It's okay, I got it!" I call through the window.

I try again, and the truck slips into reverse. And starts sliding down the hill! I slam on the brakes as Boone jumps out of the way. I almost hit him.

Adrenaline pumping, he jogs up to the window. "Do you know how to drive stick or not?"

"Yes! But this big truck is different. Just give me a second, I can do it."

"We just want to slowly let out the gravel along the road, so I can spread it as we go." He reaches inside the window, pointing out the release lever. "Just pull on this, nice and easy."

I'm extremely conscious of how near he is as he leans across me.

"At the same time you push the gas, release this lever, okay?" He's being patient with me. "You think you got it?"

I can only manage a nod. I don't like Boone to get quite this close. Or maybe I like it too much.

"I'll tell you when to go," he says, jogging back.

I check my blushing cheeks in the rearview mirror. My curls are in a low ponytail today, and I blow upward at the unruly strands that frame my face. I swear, I've only been out of the city for a couple of days and it already feels like I can see sun-streaks in my brown curls.

I whisper to my own reflection, "Stop being silly. He doesn't like you like that. And you definitely do not like him like that. Ancient history."

"OK!" he calls.

I throw it into gear again, with only a little grinding this time. I barely push the gas pedal and the clutch, while pulling the lever at the same time. The truck begins to crawl up the hill, releasing gravel bit by bit. Success! I can see in the side mirror Boone spreading it with a big shovel as we go. Progress. His muscles strain against his T-shirt as he fills in a huge pothole.

Suddenly the truck hits a spot of loose dirt and starts

slipping backward a tiny bit. Panicked, I press on the gas a bit too hard, and pull on the gravel lever too. The truck gains traction — but that makes it suddenly jolt forward! The entire load of gravel pours out of the truck in a crash of sound and dust.

"Boone!"

I throw on the emergency brake and jump out, running to the back of the truck. "Boone??"

The pile of gravel is taller than I am. Dust is everywhere, making it hard to see clearly. "BOONE!"

I start digging through the gravel with my bare hands — a fruitless attempt to move this giant pile of rock.

"Whatcha doing there, partner?"

I don't have to turn to see that Boone is standing behind me, amused. I spin around and yep, there he is — completely clean while I am covered in dust.

"That's not funny!" I say.

"It's a little funny."

"You scared me!" My voice cracks.

My fear takes the smile off Boone's face, bringing something new into his eyes. "Come on, I think we need a break," he says. And offers me a hand.

For a second, I think I won't reach out and take his hand — but turns out I can't resist.

"Tell you what," says Boone. "Why don't we walk? Leave the truck here."

* * *

We walk up Mount Baldy, which is the highest point on Goodland Farm. I'm winded but it's exhilarating to be out tramping around. Once again, I sense that flow state of my childhood creeping up — there's no clock, no schedule, no job right now — just play.

"I remember coming up here, riding Sassy," I say. The feel of that horse under me, meandering along, is strong.

"You know Sassy's still alive, right?"

"She is?!"

"Yeah, out in the back pasture where I sometimes put my horses. Granny gave her to me, years ago."

"She just gave you Sassy?" For some reason, that shocks me.

"Well, there was no one here to ride her anymore."

I feel the heat of regret sweep across me, and I concentrate on the hillside below me as I keep climbing, one foot in front of the other.

Boone sighs. "I'm sorry, I shouldn't have said that. It came out wrong."

"No, no. It's fine. And I'm glad she gave her to you, and you could take care of her."

"Believe me, your grandmother got the good end of the deal," he says, laughing a little. "That horse isn't good for much."

It's funny 'cause it's true. "Sassy is hardly a thoroughbred," I agree.

"But I love her anyway." Boone smiles at me, then changes the subject. "Hey, I'm still looking for a new place to board all my horses, by the way. I'll have 'em out of here soon."

Uncomfortable, it's my turn to change the subject. We're almost to the top of the hill. "You know, I remember this view."

"Of course you do. Still the same farm."

"It really is."

We're silent as we crest the small mountain and the countryside unfolds all around us. I can see the river snaking along one border of the property, and the back pasture where Sassy must be hanging out. I look at the various orchards, with large old apple trees planted in orderly rows but long since overgrown with weeds and untrimmed branches. I breathe it all in. Maybe Silp-Co will make it into a beautiful subdivision, where lots of people can live on this hill. But I feel a knot forming in my chest at the idea of pavement and streetlights and sewer lines dotting these pastures.

"Carly, maybe there's some way to keep it," Boone says, reading my mind. Because what else is there to think about really, except the fact that we're saying goodbye to this place.

"Boone, there isn't a way."

"You could get a loan to start, then board horses for money. Or let people lease some of the land for their other livestock. There's even a way we might get the old orchards pruned and see if they'd produce decent fruit again. I know the horses still love those apples. We just have to thin the trees out so the sunlight can reach the lower branches. It might take a couple of years, but I bet they'd start bearing again."

His face is so full of hope that I want to agree with him. But I have to come clean.

"It's not that simple, Boone. Even if I could somehow get a big loan and pay off all the back taxes, and then get this place up and running — what would I do then? This is not where my life is. I have a career back in New York."

He looks out over the hills, and I can't judge his reaction. Finally, he nods.

I charge on with my explanations and excuses. "Silp-Co has the ability to pay cash, and fast. And maybe then there's a little money left over after the taxes are paid — and I can pay you for taking care of the place the last few years."

Now he reacts, turning toward me sharply. "I don't want your money. That's not what I meant."

"I didn't mean it like that."

"How did you mean it?"

I have nothing in the way of a reply, and I don't want to say something I'll regret. I look back out at the view — and now I see Sassy, a little brown and white dot in the furthest pasture. I can't believe she's still here.

Boone turns to go. "I thought maybe I had a chance to convince you otherwise, but I see now, no matter what we do, you're selling this place to the developers." He stomps a bit of mud off one of his boots. "I promised your grandmother I'd help you when you came back. So…"

We make eye contact. Neither one of us is happy, but we've both said our piece.

"Thank you," I say, but it sounds more like *I'm sorry.*

Boone just gives me a resigned nod and leads the way back down the hill.

TEN

The next day we're back at work, spreading the huge pile of gravel with the help of wheelbarrows and shovels. It's tiring, backbreaking work and the sun gets quite hot overhead — but I pitch in and together with Boone, get a lot done. It's that sense of being helpful and working together that I love so much. After many hours, the road is definitely better. We stand back to survey our work.

"How does it look? What do you think?" I ask Boone. We haven't said much since we started working today except to coordinate our labor, so I'm not sure how he'll reply.

"Well. It looks good. But I probably need glasses."

I bump my shoulder into his. The playful teasing vibe is coming back, perhaps. Despite our differences, we can work together, right?

Boone drives the gravel truck as we head back to the house. He parks and I jump out — okay, actually I kind of limp out. My muscles are quite sore since I did quite a bit of gravel shoveling.

"Come in, for a glass of water?" I ask.

"Can't say no to that."

The kitchen is, ahem, vintage. Granny was not much of a cook, and everything here is mis-matched and frankly, adorable. I feel comfortable here — even if I can't find much in the way of drinking glasses. I settle on two vintage mason jars. Perfect. I go to fill them with fresh well water straight out of the tap — except nothing comes out. It sputters and I fiddle with the handle, but nothing. Hm, it was working this morning. I squat down and open the cabinet under the sink — and staring at me are two glowing eyes in a fuzzy face.

"AAAAAHHH!!!"

I slam the cabinet shut and rush toward the door — where I run into Boone.

"What is it?"

I point to the under-sink doors.

Boone looks downright amused. "A spider? A snake?"

"It was furry. And it looked mad."

"You have a way of inspiring that."

"Very funny. What are we going to do?"

He heads toward the cabinet doors. "Well, first of all-"

"Wait!"

He has his hand on the knob, but he doesn't open it.

"Would you rather I leave whatever it is under the sink while you sleep here tonight?"

"I'm thinking it over."

He smiles, then slowly opens the cabinet doors. I hold my breath and he points his phone flashlight inside...

An adorable small creature peers back.

"Hey there, buddy," Boone says, in that same voice he used to speak to the kitten and to Rex.

"Is that a raccoon?"

"Just a baby. Hey, little one." Boone tells me, "Prop open the back door."

As I do that, he coaxes out the little scared animal. The creature is quite irresistibly cute, to be honest. Boone murmurs calmly, persuading him to come out...

Until in a flash, the raccoon goes skittering across the floor toward the back door, which sends me screeching up on a chair.

I'm not proud about that. "I was just trying to get out of its way."

"Obviously." Boone nods. But his smile fades as he watches the baby raccoon run away. "That little one is limping badly. His back leg is really hurt."

I join him at the door, but the raccoon is soon gone, disappearing by the woodpile.

Boone shakes his head. "He's too little to be on his own like that, he should've been with his litter. I'll bet he couldn't keep up, and that's why he had to hide out by himself."

"Poor guy," I say.

"He probably won't survive on his own, with that injury."

"Wait, we have to do something."

Boone turns and gives me a look that's not teasing and not wondering and not remembering. It's something new between us, and I can't put my finger on it.

"Maybe we can do something," he says.

So Boone has a live trap in the back of his truck, because of course he does. Don't you carry around a live trap in your vehicle, just in case a stray animal needs to be doctored up? I mean, obviously.

As Boone sets the trap near the woodpile, I do the best I can to scrounge up some bait in the farmhouse kitchen.

"I found some powdered milk and mixed it with a little water," I say. "It's really old, but it has never been opened."

"That's perfect. Put some right there."

I spread a glob where he tells me. "So you just happen to have a live trap with you at all times?" I try to ask casually, as if I'm not too curious.

"It's a bit of a hobby, I guess."

"More like a calling."

He shrugs. "When I do run into critters that need a little help, this thing is completely safe — no way it could hurt the animal."

"Question is, what happens once you catch it?"

"Doctor him up, and when he's all better, let him out back here. He'll have a lot better chance of surviving if that leg's healed, and then he'll find his kind."

The trap's all set. "What now?" I ask.

"It will probably be an hour or two, maybe longer. I'll just come back tomorrow."

"I don't want that baby stuck in a cage all night," I say. "Can't you wait?"

"Sure!" Boone immediately covers for his enthusiasm. "I mean, good idea."

A moment of eye contact leaves me feeling a lot of feelings, and I think Boone is too. But what are they? I don't know mine and I can't fathom his.

I make us peanut butter and jelly sandwiches. We sit on the porch in old rocking chairs, drinking from our mason jars. It's a beautiful orchard country view, and the silence is deafening.

"Sorry all I have is water," I say.

"We could mix in some powdered milk."

"Would still be better than that coffee."

We smile and clink our water glasses. There's a breeze. I can actually smell the apple blossoms even though the closest orchard is a hundred yards away. Goodland Farm is gorgeous and kind of, I don't know, relaxing?

"I forgot how much fun I used to have out here when I was little," I say.

"What would you do?"

"Swimming of course. Jumping off the rope swing and doing flips at Blue Hole."

He looks me over, seriously. "An Olympic level diver, I'm sure."

"You know it." The smiles are easy between us. I continue on, "Sometimes after dinner, we'd make fresh peach ice cream. That was like the one thing she ever would make from scratch. Granny would turn the hand crank and I'd pour in the rock salt." The old times wash over me. "Also, she had a whole closet of dress-up clothes, just for me. Things she saved, so I could play with them. One summer she taught me to quilt — which meant she'd sew while I read Nancy Drew books. And of course we'd look at the stars at night. She'd tell me their names, but Big Dipper's about all I remember. Well, and the Little Dipper."

"Seems like you're remembering a lot, actually. What else?"

I shrug but continue. "She'd say, 'Carly you always keep your eye on the prize, but I want you to keep your eye on the skies…'" I haven't thought of that in years, and emotion creeps up on me. But I shake it off and smile. "Whatever that means! She probably just read it somewhere."

I try to chuckle, but Boone does not.

"I've never heard it before," he says. "Maybe she meant that working toward a practical goal is important, but so is following your dreams. Even if they aren't practical."

"Okay, Mister Deep Thoughts." But I smile at him.

I do find Boone surprising. No preconceived notions is right. He's grown a lot from the teenaged boy I knew for a few weeks one summer. He's gotten interesting and complicated. He was always handsome, but now there are little lines around his eyes when he smiles, and he's grown comfortable with his height. Boone Akers grew up, who would've guessed. And I need to as well.

"You know Boone, you might be right. But dreams don't pay the bills. And if I don't get a job on this next TV production that my boss, Maria, is doing, then I'm going to have to start over with someone different. Maria is the one who trained me, and we've done seven — no, eight shows together. I'm not sure I could get hired with another crew, it's pretty clique-y. And very competitive."

SNAP! And a tiny yelping sound.

"Was that —?" I turn to him.

"I think somebody's caught," says Boone, immediately heading toward the trap.

I walk tentatively behind Boone as he investigates. There's a rustling sound. All of a sudden I'm wondering what we've caught.

"You know, anything could be in that trap," I say.

Boone approaches it slowly…and suddenly jumps! Which makes me scream. Which makes him laugh. Which makes me harumph. Which makes him throw up his hands in the hey-I'm-sorry-I-thought-it-was-funny stance.

"Gotcha," he says.

"I was just worried that you scared the raccoon."

Our rapport is getting more comfortable and more playful. I won't use the f word (flirting).

Boone leans down and pulls away the brush that he piled over the trap. "Huh, I can't tell what we got."

He leaves that statement hanging. "Be careful, Boone."

"Yes, ma'am." He doesn't sound upset with my nagging though.

He pulls the cage out and there is the little raccoon, looking very scared and very cute.

"Awww," we both say in unison.

Boone wraps the adorable, docile baby raccoon in a towel and takes it into the kitchen. He examines him gently.

"Can we call him Rocky?" I ask unoriginally.

"Looks like Rocky's a she."

"Raquel then. Hello, Ms. Raquel. I can't believe she lets you hold her like that."

"She's just a young 'un, looking for a safe home. And her leg is definitely broken, poor little girl. Can you see if there's some popsicles in the freezer?"

"Baby raccoons eat three-year-old popsicles?"

"No, I want you to melt it for me. And we'll use the stick as a splint."

With the popsicle stick and my inexpert help, Boone fashions a makeshift splint for Raquel.

"Here, can you hold her?" he asks me.

"Are you sure?" She's so tiny — and also, injured — that I'm nervous.

But Boone places the baby raccoon, all wrapped in a towel, in the crook of my arm. And she seems perfectly happy.

"I'm going to mix up some of that milk and heat it up, steep some chamomile in it. That'll give her some food in her belly and help her relax too."

"Do we have tea bags?" I wonder.

"No, I'm going to pick some chamomile outside."

After he does that, Boone cuts up an old pair of rubber gloves and uses a small glass jar to make a baby bottle. "This oughta work," he says. "Here you go."

He means for me to feed the baby animal. He turns away to clean up, and I'm feeling unsure -- but I give it a try and pretty soon the sweet little raccoon latches onto the bottle and gulps it down.

"There you go!" says Boone.

"She's doing great."

"You're good at this. A really big help."

I guess that's my love language, because when he says that I'm helping, I practically feel myself glow.

Boone goes on, "But that leg will need more than a splint, I'm afraid. I'd better take her into the vet clinic in the morning for an x-ray, if they can fit her in."

Just as I am wondering if he's going to take Raquel with him tonight or leave her with me (or maybe he should stay here to take care of her?), we hear a car coming up the road. Who could that be? Boone walks to the door and I crane my neck to see Crystal, the realtor, bumping over the road entirely too quickly.

* * *

I'm still holding the raccoon and Boone's sitting next to me on the back porch. We're both listening to Crystal's report.

"So good news/bad news. Good news is Silp-Co said they'd send their CFO out to look at the property, and he's an actual decision-maker who could say, 'let's buy' — so that would cut through all the red tape."

"That's terrific," I say. Boone has no comment.

Crystal charges on. "That's what I thought too. But bad news is, he's a very busy man and he can't be here for three months."

My hope crumbles. "That'll be too late. They're going to repossess the farm."

"I could try and make some calls to other investors, but —"

Boone chimes in, "But who is going to buy a 200-acre fruit farm with no fruit for cash in the next two weeks?"

Crystal nods. "Seems pretty unlikely."

I suddenly realize something. "And you know what? Silp-Co will probably just buy it when the county auctions it off anyway."

Crystal nods. "I hate to say it, but I think you're right. Word got out. Everyone knows they can just wait, and maybe get a bargain."

This all sinks in for the first time. My eyes meet Boone's. After our long day of work on the farm road, this hits hard. What are we even doing?

"So there's really nobody that is going to want to buy this place," I say.

Crystal is full of empathy, but she has no answers. I stand and give the raccoon to Boone.

"Crystal, thank you so much for everything you have done," I say.

Crystal nods. Boone looks at the ground.

"And you too, Boone." I take a deep breath. "Looks like I'll just have to let them repossess it. No other options."

And as the sun starts to set, I look at the farmhouse that I will not be owning for much longer. I wonder if the eggs in the nest will hatch before I have to leave.

ELEVEN

The next morning, I walk down Main Street of North Haven, saying hi to everyone. A lot of faces are already looking familiar — perhaps from back in my childhood but also just from the couple of days I've been here. I see the firefighter with the dalmatian and give him a smile.

"Hey Whit, how's Rex doing?"

I stop to pet the bee-stung dog and Whit introduces me to his girlfriend — it's Celia, the radio announcer, and she remembers me from our long-ago summer friendship. They are the sweetest couple ever and I have fun chatting with them.

A couple of doors down, I notice Mr. Belichek unloading an order from a delivery truck. I run down and jump in to help.

"How's my honorary granddaughter doing?" he asks.

That gets a smile out of me, and also a little honesty. I've been giving him updates on Goodland, but this one is not fun to relay. "Not so great, Mr. B. You know we thought we'd get an offer from Silp-Co? But it is not going to happen in time. The farm is going to be repossessed for back taxes."

"You have to keep trying, Carly. There might be a way. I remember many times I thought this store wasn't going to make it. I'd fret and worry. And your granny would remind me to keep trying."

That's a sweet story, but it's just a fairy tale. I smile at him, sadly, as we unload the last box. "Thanks, Mr. Belichek. But in this case, there's really nothing left to try."

He puts a hand on my shoulder. "She believed in you."

Could he make me feel worse if he tried? But I put on a smile as I wave and walk away.

"Carly?"

I turn back toward Mr. Belichek just in time to catch the hard candy he tosses to me.

"Your granny also thought a root beer barrel could solve a lot of problems." He winks.

* * *

I decide to go check in with Samantha at the courthouse and figure out exactly what next steps are for Goodland Farms, as painful as that will be. Just as I walk into the office, Donny is leaving.

"Hi Donny. Bye Donny," I say.

Samantha waves me behind the counter to sit at the chair across from her desk.

"What was Donny doing here?" I ask with a smile.

"Oh, he brings me coffee sometimes," she says.

"I think he likes you."

"What? Donny? We're just old friends. But you know who he did have a crush on in high school? Your mother, Arlene."

"Plot twist! My mother and Donny?"

Will wonders never cease here in North Haven? This place keeps surprising me.

"But Arlene would never look his way. Barely spoke to him probably. She didn't have time for any local boys, and she couldn't wait to get out of here. But I always thought Donny liked her back then." Samantha shrugs, changing the subject. "So what can I do for you today, Miss Carly?"

"Well, you know I thought we had a buyer for Goodland Farm but turns out they can't come for at least three months. So I just thought I'd check — is there any possible way we could delay the foreclosure?"

"Oh sweetie, you have owed for so long. And then the penalties and interest on top of that. Unless someone's a nonprofit, there's nothing they can ever do to stop this process. I've seen it before." Her manner conveys complete hopelessness.

"I knew it was a long shot, just thought I'd ask."

I realize that I have been carrying a tiny bit of hope around in my heart, but now that is officially gone.

Samantha is full of empathy. "Maybe you could get a loan. Pay down the minimum, just until you can sell?"

Samantha hands me the paperwork, and when I see the exact figures, I am crestfallen and completely resigned.

"There's no way I can qualify for a loan that size. And it would just be delaying the inevitable. I feel so dumb! How did I not know I was supposed to do this?"

"Honey, there were so many notices sent. You have to open your mail."

"Notices? What notices?"

Samantha looks at me like I'm a little nuts. "The delinquent property tax letters," she says. "Those envelopes with big red *urgent* on the outside?"

"I never got any. To what address?"

"Let's see." Samantha flips through the file and looks it up. "Certified delivery. Carly Walton. 134 East 62nd, Apartment 1709."

"That's my mother's place," I say.

Samantha and I look at each other, and I realize my mouth is hanging open.

"I guess Arlene didn't give them to you," she says.

Could that be true?

* * *

I'm outside the courthouse, pacing around the town

square. My blood is coursing with adrenaline or cortisol or whichever is the not-feel-good-chemical. Fight or flight, but there's nowhere to go, so I'm going to call Mom. I've got to know the truth. What should I say? I'll just be honest. I take out my phone and scroll to the "Mom" contact and as I am about to push the button —

My phone rings. It's a FaceTime, from Maria.

I change gears emotionally, and answer.

"Maria, hello! How are you?"

Dramatically as always, she says, "Horrible. Help. Please."

I have to laugh. "Okay, of course. I'd love to help, you know that. What's up?"

"Well, first of all, you should know — Rupert hired me for the TV series. Solo. I'm sorry."

I'm crushed inside. But I try to put on a brave face. "No worries. That's great. I'm happy for you!"

Maria is walking through Manhattan as she talks, and she frowns at people who get in her way. "Well, it *would* be great if I had something to show him. The whole series is set at a house out in the country, and the Buckner estate location that I showed him fell through."

"You mean the Smith Victorian?"

"Yes! It's only our biggest set on the whole show, where all the main action takes place. And I've got nothing else to show him."

"Call the Deckers-"

"Already did."

My wheels are turning. Scouting locations and finding the perfect place is fairly difficult but finding an ideal house that has property owners who are willing to rent out to a movie company can be almost impossible.

"How about the farm upstate, that belongs to those people with the llamas?" I say.

She shakes her head vehemently. "Carly, I've tried everything! Rupert and I are supposed to scout again on Friday and I am telling you, I have absolutely nothing to show him."

My wheels are turning. "Maria, tell me exactly what you're looking for."

* * *

I see Boone's truck parked outside the veterinarian office and I know he's taken in Raquel, so I decide to make a quick stop. I bustle inside and find the receptionist, Irene, talking to a man holding a box of rambunctious stray puppies that were abandoned.

"I'm sorry," says Irene. "There are no animal shelters available for stray dogs right now. So many puppies, but everything in the county is full. You can try going across the state border into Massachusetts. They might have something?"

As the disappointed gentleman leaves, Irene turns to me.

"How can I help you?"

"I was in here the other day, with Boone Akers. I was wondering if he's here? I think he was bringing in our — I mean, his baby raccoon?"

"Oh yes, he's here. Boone's always bringing in one critter or another." She rolls her eyes lovingly as she points the way.

I find Boone caring for the little raccoon in the back room, which is still full of other recuperating animals in crates and cages. I'm stopped short looking at this big man being so tender with little Raquel. Why does he have to do that in front of me? My insides go ooey-gooey.

He notices me and smiles. "Hey, good news. Our little Rocky-Raquel is already better. With the cast on, she's barely limping." But then a slight sadness creeps into his face. "I was thinking, I'd like to let her go out at Goodland Farm before the place is repossessed."

"Boone-"

"I just mean, it'll be so much easier for her to get acclimated to living on her own, in a place that she knows."

"Yes, of course. About that. I have news."

"What is it?"

"I might have another plan."

He's not enthused. "So what now, another developer's going to swoop in and get it?"

I shake my head, smiling. Boone is reluctantly encouraged. "Let's let this little girl have some time outside. We can talk there."

He scoops up Raquel and hands her to me. Once we're

back out on Main Street in the beautiful springtime air, Boone says, "I'm listening."

I give him a big smile. "You know the movie production company?"

"They hired you back? That's great, Carly."

My excitement is tamped down for a second. "No. I didn't get the job."

"Oh, I'm sorry," says Boone.

"Who knows, maybe it was for the best."

"Maybe it was for the best," he says. "Because you've found your true calling as a gravel truck driver?"

I laugh, then look at him shyly. From his smile, I'd say we both are feeling the significance of what's been happening since I've been here. Not sure what that is exactly, but we both feel the significance. We arrive at the little park that's a block from the vet's office and I gingerly set Raquel in the grass so she can get some fresh air and sunshine.

"Boone, the film company lost their main house location. They need a place to shoot out in the country, with lots of parking around it for all their trucks. It has to be on a hill with a long view, just like Goodland."

He's already skeptical. "So they want to film here?"

"Well, not yet. But the director, Rupert, is going to come scout. And if he likes it — Boone, they pay a lot per day. In just a few weeks of shooting, I could make a dent in the back taxes. A big dent. Start paying them off. This might actually be a way to save the farm."

Boone is deep in thought. He's very sincere when he says, "That sounds great, Carly."

A beat, as we realize the possibilities.

"Do you really think you can do it?" he says.

"It's not a done deal yet. And I can't do it alone. This is not like Silp-Co, these people will be looking at the actual house, not just a gravel road. And that old farmhouse needs to be fixed up quite a bit, at least so it looks cozy and comfortable. Maria said they're looking for 'upscale farm chic' apparently. I don't know exactly what that means."

Boone shrugs, considering. "A little shiplap, a few signs that say *blessed*, maybe some reclaimed wood shelving."

"Okay…"

Boone tilts his head. "Actually that might be a bit more modern ranch than farm chic."

"Who are you right now?!" I say.

"Just a boy. Standing in front of a girl. Who likes home décor TV."

I smack him playfully. "No preconceived notions."

"That's right."

We smile, looking deeply into each other's eyes. Energized by the plan — and by each other.

"Okay," I say. "If we're going to convince Rupert, it will have to be perfect. And that means not just cleaning and decluttering, but also surface repairs and landscaping so it looks fresh and-"

"Slow down now. They're not here yet."

I take a deep breath. "Obviously, I can't do this alone. Boone, please, will you help me?"

"I don't know too much about movie companies—"

"That's my specialty!"

"But I do know that your granny would want me to do anything I could to help save Goodland Farm."

"Even drink my coffee?"

"I mean, let's be reasonable."

"Thank you so much, Boone." And I say it like I really, really mean it. Because I really, really mean it.

Boone shrugs. "Let's get Rocky-Raquel settled at the vet, then we'll go."

TWELVE

We don't waste any time. We get a bunch of cleaning supplies and things we'll need at Belichek's General Store on the way out of town. I head out to the farm and Boone goes to his house to pick up tools.

By mid-afternoon, I'm scrubbing the windows while Boone replaces a little patch of wobbly flooring. There are already drop cloths and tools and messes that attest to our hours of work.

"There!" I say. "Amazing what some window cleaner can do."

"Especially when you get it on the windows instead of your yoga clothes."

"I'm plum tired," I say, wiping my brow with the back of my hand. "Okay, now I'm actually turning into Granny."

Boone laughs. "That did sound like her."

"On to the kitchen!" I pick up my cleaning bucket and

wince a little at how heavy it is. My arms are getting sore.

"Hey, maybe we should take a break," says Boone.

"PB&J for lunch coming up."

"I have a better idea. Come on."

Boone drives me in his pick-up through the farm, over the now-fairly-level gravel road. When he turns on his radio, it's once again Carly Rae Jepsen bopping along, giving out her phone number so someone will "Call Me Maybe."

"What are the chances of us hearing this song twice?" I wonder.

Boone shrugs. "Pretty high, considering it's a playlist."

I have to laugh. "You put her your playlist? I mean granted, it's the world's catchiest song, but—"

"This compilation is from back in the day. It's got a lot of golden oldies on it."

Something sweeps over me — maybe I'm thrilled, or maybe I'm panicked. Boone has a playlist from the exact summer that he and I dated for a few weeks? And he's been listening to it for all these years? As if on cue, "Call Me Maybe" ends and Bruno Mars starts singing about how he'd catch a grenade for you. This is one we heard back then as well. Is that a little, um, creepy?

Boone says. "This was the year I went away to college, so all of these songs still kind of resonate with me."

And just as fast as I was worried that he was obsessed with me, now I am devastated that these songs have nothing to do with me. But it's like Boone can read my mind.

"Of course, that's not the only thing that happened that year." He winks at me.

We pull off the regular road and drive across the pasture, then he puts it in park and opens his door.

"Are we going to Blue Hole?" I ask. "I don't have a bathing suit."

"Water's probably still too cold anyway. We're just going to have a look."

It's an enchantingly, achingly beautiful swimming spot. The creek widens and slows right here, surrounded by huge elm trees with tangled roots that line the bank. It's shady and quiet and the only sound is the soft gurgle of the creek. We are a world away from anything else.

"Is it just like you remember it?" Boone asks.

"Actually, I think I'd forgotten how beautiful it is. I haven't been to this place for many years. After I quit spending summers here, I only came back a couple of times to visit." I feel some tears threatening.

"This place really is special," Boone whispers reverently, like he's in a church.

We stand in awe, surrounded by these old growth trees and the clearest, sparkliest water imaginable. How is it that I may have let this magical spot slip through my fingers?

"I hope Rupert likes it," I say. "Great place for shooting."

Boone doesn't chime in on that topic, and I feel like I just ruined the mood.

"Where's the rope swing?" I ask.

"Rope? I've never seen that. I don't think there is one anymore."

I go to the bottom of the biggest, oldest elm and peer upward. "Are you sure about that?" I ask.

"I've been caretaking at Goodland for several years now, and more than once I'd come over here in the middle of a summer day for a swim. I've never seen a rope swing in all that time."

I start to climb that big tree, picking my way upward, branch to branch. "I used to do back flips," I say.

"That sounds like a long time ago."

"What, you don't think I can do it anymore?"

Boone's getting nervous. "Of course you can," he says, placating me.

"You think I'm going to fall for that reverse psychology? You don't think I can do it."

My foot slips a tiny bit and Boone takes in his breath sharply, but I quickly regain my hold on the elm branches.

"Carly, I'm serious. You're getting pretty high up there. Come on down."

But I climb even further, into an upper crevice of the tree. "There it is! I told you!" I point above my head. The rope swing has been looped over a branch and tucked out of sight.

"Well, look at that," says Boone, not at all excited. "A rope. You were right! You can come on down."

"Now I can show you my mad skills."

"I hope you're kidding."

I reach over my head and grab the rope. I know it must look scary from way down there, but I honestly have a pretty secure foothold in the tree's upper branches. Besides, I did this a million times when I was a kid. I arrange my hands on the rope, just like I used to.

"One...Two..."

"Carly. I'm serious." Boone does not sound happy.

"Three!"

I jump off the tree and hold onto the rope, swinging way out in a big arc over the creek. I let go just when I'm at the peak — and I get a glimpse of Boone's wide eyes — but instead of doing a flip, I strike a silly pose in mid-air and land in a big cannonball splash.

Without coming up for air, I swim underwater to the far side of Blue Hole. When I finally lift my head above surface, I see that Boone has waded in to his knees and is calling my name.

"Carly!"

But I'm behind him.

"Whatcha doing there, partner?" I say.

He spins around to see me in the water near the opposite bank.

"That is not funny," he says.

"Maybe a little funny?"

In the smile that we share right then, with my curls dripping around my face and with true relief flooding his, a real moment passes between us. Of the we-like-each-other variety.

Boone helps me out of the water and luckily my tank top and shorts are the type that dry quickly. Lululemon may not be the best for doing home repairs, but it does not let me down during this impromptu swim.

Boone has brought a knapsack and he pulls out a sandwich.

"Look at that," I say. "You brought your lunch?"

"I brought our lunch."

"Color me impressed. What is it?"

"Caprese on a baguette."

"What?"

"It's mozzarella and tomato, with a drizzle of olive oil and some balsamic reduction."

"I know what caprese is. I'm just…"

"Just a little bit full of preconceived notions?"

"Just wondering where the fresh basil is."

Boone's smile is wide and he doesn't break eye contact. We're sitting so close, side by side on a soft mossy spot on the bank. I have goosebumps, but it must be because I'm still wet from my swim and there's a spring breeze blowing. He leans his face to mine and I tilt my chin up toward him. I swear he's staring at my lips for, like, ten seconds — and then he pulls back. He pulls out half of the sandwich and hands it to me.

"Oh, there's definitely basil in there," he says.

* * *

WHAT HAPPENED TO MY EX

We finish up our picnic and are lying back comfortably, full and happy, looking up at the dappled sunlight coming through the leaves. There's a calm that's overtaken us, probably because we're at this magical little swimming hole, but possibly because we're together and that feels good too.

"So you grew up in North Haven, right?" I realize I don't know that much about Boone, even though we had a sweet summer fling all those years ago. To be honest, as a kid I hadn't thought to ask about his back story.

"Yes but no," Boone says. "My father was a rodeo cowboy, remember? So even though I'm from here, we were on the road pretty much ten months a year. Place to place. Rambling life. I always wanted to grow roots when I was little, but…"

"But at some point, maybe it's too late to grow roots?"

"No. That's not what I meant."

I decide to change the subject. "What about your mom, couldn't you stay with her while your dad traveled?"

"Never knew her. Or at least not that I remember. She ran off when I was a baby. Dad never got over it, exactly. Anyway it was just me and him, on the rodeo circuit. Traveling town to town. He was a calf roper. I took care of his horses. That was our bread and butter — his winnings at rodeos, and a lot of that was dependent on his horse."

"Animals loved you even then."

Boone shrugs. I don't think he loves talking about himself. "That was a long time ago," he says. "Dad wound up getting hurt, couldn't work, and we eventually lost our land. Then he passed not long after I went to college."

"I remember. I'm so sorry."

"He had been sick awhile although he'd never admit it." Boone lifts up on one elbow and looks at me. "Carly, if I had a piece of land like this, I'd never sell it. I hope you can hang onto it."

I look around this incredible watering hole, the majestic trees.

"I know what you mean."

He lies back down. "I'd just stay out here alone forever," he says.

"Alone? Is that what you want?"

"I'm not sure it's a matter of what I want. I've always been a loner. That's the way it wound up. That's what got me into farm work."

"What about a family? I mean, someday."

"I saw my father go through too much after he lost my mom… I'd be so content out here though. Have a few animals. I mean, look around. What more do you need in life?"

I'm touched. I gaze up at the sunlight flickering through the tall branches and hear the gentle gurgling of the creek like a lullaby. It really is magic. But I wonder if I might need more. My mom has instilled career in me for so many years, there's no way I could walk away from that.

* * *

The next two days are long hours of painting and cleaning and repairing. Sometimes it feels like we are just making more of a mess than ever, but a bit of the progress comes through. It's a surface makeover, so everything is good for the cameras. And the shiny surface is looking pretty good.

The sun is about to set on our last day of work, when I tag along with Boone as he walks to the barn to feed the horses. They are beyond thrilled to see him, naturally. He fills the trough with fresh water and throws a mound of hay out in the pasture as they meander over to eat. Crickets chirp. A breeze blows. The stars glow up one by one. The feeling I have fills me to the brim.

"Look who's joining us," Boone says.

It's Sassy. She may be older now, but she's a beautiful sight.

"Sassy!" I reunite with this long-lost friend, giving her a hug. It's almost like I can feel Granny's presence, and how she used to lift me up on this pony when I was a girl.

"It's amazing," I say, running my hands over Sassy's neck. "How it all comes back to me — the smells, the sounds, the feel of her coat. It's like Granny's still here, in a way."

I realize Boone's looking at me, and I get shy.

"Here," he says, handing me a carrot from his pocket.

"How long have you been carrying this around?" I laugh. "You are such a Boy Scout. Always prepared."

We watch Sassy munch on the carrot, eating the whole

thing slowly like a dignified old lady. She loves it.

"Carly, can I ask you something? Why'd you ever quit coming out here?"

"Wasn't my choice really. Once I turned seventeen, my mom wanted me to work. I got a counselor job at a summer camp."

"What could be a better summer camp than this?"

"Right?! Instead, I worked at this ritzy place with air-conditioned bunks where you could only ride English saddles or go out on sailboats. We did Pilates."

"I love Pilates, it's great for rehabbing injuries," says Boone. "But I never would've figured you for someone who went to rich kids' camp."

"Mom said it was a 'networking opportunity.'"

"What sixteen-year-old needs to network?"

"I was seventeen." He rolls his eyes and I become a little defensive. He's never even met my mother. "You don't understand. Mom wanted more for me. She's a businesswoman, very hardworking. She's had a lot of success."

I watch Sassy walk away, toward the other horses.

"I get that," says Boone.

"I have to make my mom proud. She's worked too hard for me to — OH!"

I point at the almost-dark sky. A meteor streaks across, then another. It's magnificent and mysterious.

"Oh, that's right," says Boone. "The Perseids are this month."

Two more sparkling fireballs fall across the sky, almost surreal against the Vermont twilight.

"So beautiful," I say.

"Yes, very beautiful."

But he means something else, and I know it. I turn to him. I can see a bit of that starlight in his eyes, lighting up the flecks of gold. He looks at me so tenderly, and under his gaze I find myself getting emotional.

"Are you okay?"

What is going on with me? Why are all these big feelings bubbling up inside me that I can't name?

"It's just — the meteors surprised me," I say.

"And you surprise me."

The jolt passes back and forth between us, we both feel it. The attraction between us in this moment, out in the spring breeze, with the horses nearby, standing under the stars as they pop out one by one — it's undeniable.

Boone leans over just as I lift up on tiptoe. Our mouths meet gently, both of us asking a silent question: should we? Our bodies tell us overwhelmingly: yes, you should. His hands reach for my waist, pulling me closer.

A rustling in the bushes — and not just a small sound, either. I jump, now on high alert.

"What was that?"

"Probably just a possum," Boone says. "Or a bear."

"What!"

Boone laughs. "We're fine."

But he's making fun of me, and I'm suddenly back to

being my Manhattan-career-girl self. "We'd better get back. Big day tomorrow before Rupert gets here."

Boone nods. I already regret ruining the moment, but it's too late now.

THIRTEEN

I wake up to a beautiful morning, feeling a little nervous about Maria and Rupert showing up. I hope I haven't oversold this place, telling them it was a perfect location. It would be an enormous undertaking to bring a whole shooting crew to little North Haven, but if they like this place enough, they will.

I'm out on the porch looking at the birds' nest (still nothing hatched) when Boone pulls up. He brought us coffee from Cake My Day — extra-large cups, at that. We don't sip, we gulp — and get to work with all the last minute fix-ups. I'm finishing planting flowers in the front bed and Boone is sweeping the porch when my phone dings.

"It's Maria. She and Rupert are almost here."

I wish I felt more confident. I stand up and brush off my jeans, take a step back and look at the farmhouse with a critical eye. What would I think of this place if I were a British film director who was about to shoot an entire limited series for Netflix? Actually, the place is awfully charming and in an incredibly picturesque spot.

"I guess we've done about all we can for now," says Boone.

"I can't believe how much we accomplished. Thank you so much." I think about kissing him again, but neither one of us has tried that since last night. I dart up on the porch and adjust a decorative pillow on the rocking chair.

"It does look good," Boone says. "But it's all surface stuff. We didn't address the electrical panel or upgrade the plumbing —"

"That doesn't matter, all they care about are appearances."

Boone raises an eyebrow at that.

I explain further, "They'll bring an outside generator for the power, and a honeywagon for the plumbing. Looks are everything on film."

"So you keep saying."

The car with Maria and Rupert is pulling up now. I take a deep breath and hear my mother saying *Posture, Carly!*

"I guess I'll be going," says Boone.

"What? No. Stay, please!" I'm a little embarrassed by how needy I sound, so I tone it down a bit. "I mean, you know so much about the place."

"I think you know a lot more about this place than you give yourself credit for."

"Boone, I'm nervous."

"Why? This is just the man who fired you from your job in front of a room full of people in a very embarrassing way, who's now come all the way out to Vermont to judge your entire house."

"You're right. I feel so much better."

But I am laughing as Maria and Rupert get out of their car. Boone and I walk over to meet them.

"Hello!" Maria air kisses me on both cheeks, rather extravagantly.

"Maria, Rupert, hello!" I say.

Rupert has his nose in the air, already judging his surroundings. "Carly," he says, then turns to Boone: "And you are?"

I feel very eager to please, thrown back into this old work dynamic. "Rupert, this is Boone Akers. He's the — the farm foreman actually."

Boone puts out his hand to shake, with a smile. "Sounds like I just got a promotion. How do you do?"

Rupert likes to be the most charming man in a room. He shakes hands and sniffs. "Show me around already."

Boone leads the way and Rupert follows. Maria comes to me and whispers, "So who's the cute farmhand? Why didn't you tell me?"

"He's just been helping me fix up things. An old friend."

She watches Boone up ahead, starting to show Rupert things. "So he's available?"

I'm taken aback by the question. "Of course. I mean, I don't know. He could be dating someone. I didn't ask."

Maria is already walking up to Boone. She takes his arm and nods as he talks. I'm so surprised by how rattled I am. Maria's always flirting; it's just her way. I try to brush it off.

"Shall we go inside?" I ask, keeping my voice bright.

As I show Rupert and Maria around the interior, Boone hangs back, watching me. I feel my genuine enthusiasm for the house building up. "I know you were looking for a real country kitchen, and I think this could qualify. This is a very old wood-burning stove that's still in working order."

Rupert gives it a glance. "Hmm, that might work. But we'd have to hook it up to gas, so the flame would be constant. We could rewire it though."

Boone speaks up, surprising us. "That's a vintage stove. If you hook it up to gas, it will lose its original integrity-"

"It will be fine!" I jump in.

Boone reacts at being interrupted. He looks at me and throws up his hands like, okay, fine.

I move on. "And this next room could be perfect for the den scenes with the family characters."

Rupert looks around the area, with its dark wood beams and original timber walls. "Possibly. The room size is right. And the windows are okay."

Maria and I exchange hopeful looks behind Rupert's back.

"But all of this would need to be brightened up, obviously," he continues. "A nice coat of paint — make it all white."

"Sure…" I say. "It can be painted.

"Especially these log walls."

Boone speaks up. "Those are the original timbers, hand hewn in the 1870s."

Rupert is not used to getting pushback. "We're not going to hurt them. Just lighten up all this dark wood. And paint over that stone wall too. It will look great. Modernize the design!" Rupert's finally getting enthused. "Yeah, I can start to see it now."

Boone can't hold his tongue. "The stone wall is chisel-cut masonry, with every piece hauled in and fit together by hand. And these beams are old-growth pine, you can't get this stuff anymore."

I try to placate him. "It's fine, we can paint it and then sand it off after filming."

Rupert laughs. "Don't worry, it will look fabulous painted. You won't want to sand it off! You'll see."

Maria agrees. "Yes, upscale farm chic. I would love to see it all white in here."

Boone stands firm. "I'm just saying, if you paint that wood, it will never have its original patina again. And you could never sand it all off anyway."

"What do you think, Carly?" Rupert turns to me.

A moment of truth — everyone looks to me. Boone especially.

I take a deep breath. "Sure, we can paint everything. Of course. It should be fine."

Rupert is triumphant. He even comes over and gives me an air kiss. "I'm so glad you thought to show me this place, Carly. Really helpful. I forgot how good you are at this kind of work."

I feel the glow of approval, and it sounds to me like this might really happen. Rupert and Maria move on to the next room.

I speak quietly, urgently, to Boone. "Hey, what are you doing?"

"Just talking about the farmhouse."

"Boone, I am doing whatever has to be done to save this house."

"Are things worth saving if they can't stay true to themselves?" He stares at me intently, waiting for a serious answer.

"It's better to get something than nothing," I say. "I don't want to lose Goodland completely."

* * *

The full tour of the house and surrounding land takes a long time, and that's a good thing. Because the more questions Rupert asks, the more interested he is, and the slower we go. We wind up at Blue Hole, and it bowls them over.

"Oh my gosh!" Maria gasps. "I can't believe how

gorgeous this is! So unspoiled and peaceful."

Rupert strides around, clearly excited. "It will be a battle scene, and we can put one side over there — and the ambush overtakes them!"

"What kind of movie is this?" Boone wonders.

Rupert takes a haughty tone. "A modern reimagining of something called *Rashomon*."

Boone smiles slowly, unperturbed. "You mean the Japanese samurai film from the 1950s?"

That is the last thing Rupert expected to hear. "Uh, yes," he says. "That's the one."

Boone nods. "I like those alternating character perspectives. Interesting film."

Rupert is speechless. I have to turn away to hide my smile.

"Let's go look on that side!" Maria pipes up.

I let them lead the way. As Boone walks by me, I whisper, "Preconceived notions." I think that will get a smile out of him — but he just keeps on walking.

Once we get to the other side of Blue Hole, the view is even more spectacular — mossy elms shading us, the pure spring water sparkling. Maria has pulled Boone into a sidebar conversation and she keeps giggling and touching his arm.

I concentrate on giving Rupert the tour. "This water is from a natural spring that comes up not far from here. Sixty-eight degrees year-round."

"You can't see temperature on film, Carly," says Rupert.

"No, of course not. Just fun facts."

"We'd have to cut down that ugly rope, of course," he muses.

I look up at my childhood rope swing. Hours of climbing up and jumping off of it, over and over. Boone and Maria have walked over and are listening now.

"Actually, you can just tuck it up into the tree and it's practically invisible," I say.

Rupert scoffs. "Practically invisible is not good enough. I need a working atmosphere that is conducive to my creativity!"

That sounds familiar. It's the same thing Rupert said when he brought that dog into Ms. Shawcross' apartment. Boone watches me carefully.

I take a deep breath. "I assure you, it won't hurt a thing to leave up the rope swing."

Rupert furrows his brow. "It's almost like you don't want us to shoot here. The filming has to take precedence over everything, Carly, do you understand? Certainly over a little thing like a rope swing that needs to be cut down. As a matter of fact, we may have to cut down some of these trees."

"Cut them down completely? Not the big elms?"

"The battle needs a big clearing along the water."

Maria nods at me, widening her eyes. More decision time. This is an impossible choice, between horrible and terrible.

"Of course," I say. "If it turns out you absolutely need to."

"Great!" Rupert walks on.

Maria sidles up, giving my arm a squeeze. "You sure that will be okay?"

I nod despite my real feelings. "Maybe we'll figure out a way that doesn't have to happen."

"Sure, hon," she says, moving after Rupert.

Boone's very disappointed. I know that. That's why I don't look at him for the rest of the tour.

* * *

When Rupert and Maria are about to leave, Boone and I see them off, walking them to their car.

Rupert stops and gives me a serious look. "Carly, I'm liking this place. I think it might work."

"That's wonderful!" I say.

"I said I *think*. Let's talk about it tonight. All of us. You can even bring your farmhand," he says, half kidding. "Or your boyfriend?"

"Oh no, um, he's-"

"No," Boone says firmly to the idea we are dating. It kills me, but what did I expect?

A quick but awkward silence follows.

"Where should we meet tonight?" says Maria, saving the conversation.

"What's the nicest place in town, Boone?" asks Rupert.

Maria says, "I saw a sign in town for something — the Apple Blossom Festival?"

I hedge. "Oh, is that tonight? I'm not sure if you'd want to do that."

"What is it?" Maria asks Boone.

"Dancing, food, just us locals having an annual get-together. Celebrating where we live."

"There's a great casual café, called Cake My Day —"

"They'll be closed during the festival," Boone tells me.

Rupert opens his car door. "I love a little local color. Apple Blossom Festival it is."

Once Boone and I are alone, there's undeniable tension. I don't know what to say, and I guess he doesn't either.

"Well, that went pretty well," I say.

Boone walks to the porch and stands on his tiptoes, looking at the birds' nest. "Still haven't hatched. Hope they can before all of this gets *painted*."

"Boone, listen-"

"No, I get it." He puts a hand up to stop my explanations and rationalizations. "I understand, lesser evils and all that. Right now, I have to do something."

He walks to his truck and I follow him, thinking he's about to leave — but instead he pulls out a little crate. It's Raquel the raccoon, and she no longer has her little leg cast.

"Oh cutie! Is she all better, you think?"

He gives me a nod and carries the pen toward the woodpile.

"Are you sure she's ready?" I ask.

"The sooner she's back in her element, the better. And I want to do it before the movie company — or whoever — comes in and starts tearing things up."

He sets the cage down gingerly and opens it. We watch as the raccoon tentatively looks out. I feel a lump in my throat.

"Go ahead, Raquel," I say. "Go home. You belong here."

Looking adorable, the little critter hesitates and sniffs the air. She jumps out, almost like a bunny, then gleefully bounds away. Why am I feeling so emotional over this?

"They grow up so fast," says Boone.

I laugh and he smiles a little, his mood softening. He kicks the dirt and says, "So you think it went well today, huh?"

"Boone, you know I'm just trying to save the farm. Let's not lose sight of that."

"I know. But tell me this, Carly: why are you trying to save it? So you can sell it to Silp-Co next year for more money? Or so you can leave it empty for another three years and never even visit your grandmother's house?"

"That's not fair."

"Maybe it's not fair." He stares deeply into my eyes, taking a step closer. "But I can't help how I feel about this place. And just — everything."

"HELLO?" a female voice calls out from the front of the house.

"Oh my god," I say.

"What?"

I look at Boone, wide-eyed. "That's my mother."

* * *

Boone leaves quickly and I'm grateful for that. Mom and I wave goodbye to him as he pulls away.

She starts in immediately. "I know he's handsome, but I hope you don't think you actually like a local boy."

"Mom, please."

"Call it a mother's intuition, but I thought I could sense something between you two."

"In the time it took him to walk around the house and leave?"

She shrugs, giving me a look that says, *well?*

"I've only known Boone for a little over a week. Well, I mean — that's not true. I knew him way back when-"

"I knew it!"

"Briefly! We went out a few times, when we were teenagers. He's just been helping me out around here, cleaning everything up."

"Well, I don't want you to think you belong here, with someone like that. You are destined for much greater things than North Haven."

"Please stop it." Something in my tone of voice alerts her to my seriousness. "Now I have to ask you something,

Mom. Did you ever get tax notices in the mail? Addressed to me, for the property taxes on this farm?"

"I get so much junk mail, I have no idea, Carly. Aren't you going to offer me some iced tea?"

I feel my heart racing. I don't know if I've ever really confronted her like this before. "Mother, why didn't you give those to me?!"

She is caught. I see her weighing her options and deciding to come clean. There's not a bit of regret in her voice when she tells me, "I didn't give you those tax notices because I didn't want you to have to pay money for this old broken-down place. It was foisted upon you just like it was foisted upon me. We don't belong here, Carly. You don't belong here."

"That was not your decision to make!"

"I always just want the best for you, honey. You have such an exciting career and you're going to do great things." She shrugs and smiles. "I know I did the right thing. I love you more than anything in the world, and I always want the best for you."

How can I argue with that? I'm incredibly angry but I also know my mother loves me. Why is family stuff so confusing? "Look, Mom, you do not get to dictate my life!"

She puts a loving hand over mine, her eyes full of vulnerability — something I rarely see in her. "Carly, this country town is not for you. It's a black hole and I want you to be free of it."

"I don't think North Haven is like you remember it."

"Oh, I'm pretty sure it is. Nothing changes in a place like this."

"Why don't you come to the Apple Blossom Festival with me tonight and see?"

FOURTEEN

I look through the "dress-up closet" that Granny always let me play in, and it's full of wonderful vintage clothes. It's better than any curated thrift shop in Manhattan, that's for sure. The clothes have been covered in plastic and bars of soap are stuck in there, keeping it all fresh. Everything in the closet seems to be my size. I slip on a summer dress in a beautiful shade of pink, a lot like the apple blossoms that should be blooming any day now. It fits like a glove.

Mom steps into the room to see. "That was mine, years ago."

"I used to play dress up with all of these clothes."

"And now you've grown into them."

"It's funny how they kind of fit me perfectly. Where did you wear this dress?"

She sighs deeply. "I wore it the night I first danced with your father."

It gives me a start, just hearing that word *father*. Arlene never, ever brings up the subject herself, and I know barely anything about him. I don't want to break the spell, so I just say casually, "Oh really?"

Mom sits on the bed, looking at me in her old dress. "He was the most handsome boy I ever met. He was from Chicago, here visiting his cousins. We were married within a month — love at first dance, we used to say. Then he got a great job, working as an apprentice lineman for Con Ed in Illinois. Good money. After a while, he applied for a position in New York, because he knew that was my dream." She smiles softly and stares off into the distance. "We moved to Manhattan, a tiny little apartment, and we had you. Everything seemed to be working out. And then."

She pauses. I realize I've been barely breathing. "The accident," I say.

She nods. "A big storm. The power was out all over, there were high winds and —" She decides to avoid the details, and just shakes her head. "They said the anchor cables snapped. It was a fluke thing."

She wipes away a tear. I can hardly ever remember seeing my mother cry. She might get misty at the end of a movie or something, but her general demeanor is always one-foot-in-front-of-the-other optimism. I sit next to her on the bed, putting an arm around her, laying my head on her shoulder.

She squeezes my knee and continues, "That's when I knew I had to support us. You were just a tiny infant. But it was me and you. Carly, don't throw away all my work to make a better life for you."

"I won't, Mom."

"You deserve something better than this old shack in the middle of nowhere!"

We fall into a hug, both of us full of conflicted emotions. I know that she loves me. "I love you, Mom."

"I have to fix my makeup," she says and hurries out of the room.

I hear something outside the bedroom window and go to investigate. Three tiny baby birds poke their beaks upward, squeaking for food. The mama swoops into the nest and gives them each something to eat.

Symbolism much?

* * *

By the time we get to the Apple Blossom Festival, it's already hopping. Mom gets a work call and wanders off to answer it.

North Haven looks so festive tonight, the town's all shiny and happy. I'm a little worried that I'm overdressed in the delicate vintage dress I finally settled on wearing, a robin's egg blue linen, edged with white eyelet. But I quickly see that there are people dressed up even more than me, and some less. Come one, come all. It's a street dance party for all ages, with lights strung across the town square. There are bales of hay to sit on and a band of local teenagers with two fiddlers and a lot of enthusiasm. They sound great. Everyone's having a good time, from the two little boys having a light saber fight with sticks, to the couple in their nineties on the dance floor.

And then I see Boone and I realize that's what I've been looking for the whole time. He's talking to Mr. Belichek and I wave to both of them. Despite myself, I feel my heart soar at the sight of Boone. I feel a little self-conscious that I've let my curls fall free around my shoulders and have put on a bit of lipstick and this shimmery dress that blows in the spring breeze. Am I trying too hard? He turns away from me, continuing his talk with Mr. B.

I notice a table where a couple of people are serving cups of apple cider, and I pitch in to help. There are apple cider donuts too, and baked apple chips covered in fresh ground cinnamon. The line is long and I can see Boone is in it, just a few more people in front of him before he gets to me. I smile at him and he makes a joking impatient face, tapping his wrist like I'm taking a long time. I have to laugh.

"Carly, darling!" It's Rupert, just arriving. He walks straight to the front of the line. "Show me around! Isn't this just adorable?" He grabs a cup of cider and walks away. I hurry to follow him.

"Yes, isn't it lovely?" I say.

"It's like a picture postcard. But this town is probably too small to have their own postcard."

116

I glance back at Boone, seeing the disappointment in his face. He actually steps out of line, not even waiting for food anymore. But I need to focus on my work right now.

"Rupert, let me show you around. North Haven would be an incredible place to shoot a film." Out of the corner of my eye, I see Maria walking up to chat with Boone.

As I walk Rupert around, showing him the small town sights and introducing him to the people that I know, he is not-so-subtly insulting townspeople one by one:

"So besides this, is there anything people do for fun around here?"

or

"I just can't believe this good wine was made here."

or, my favorite (not):

"You seem smart, did you go to school here?"

I'm embarrassed, but I try to cover for him. "Rupert's not familiar with many parts of America," I say. "He's still getting to know this country."

The townspeople are a little nonplussed, and mostly disinterested in his rudeness. There's too much other fun to be had tonight. I find myself hoping that when the film crew arrives (if we're lucky enough to lock down this deal), that all will go well.

Rupert excuses himself for "the little boys' room" and I walk toward my mother. She sits alone by the bandstand nursing a drink, and Mr. Belichek walks up to her. They start talking before they notice me.

"I'm surprised to see you here, Arlene," he says.

"I only came to town to make sure Carly gets rid of that farm. I don't want the responsibility hanging over her."

Mr. Belichek nods. "Family is a responsibility, you're right. But maybe that's not a bad thing. What else makes life worth living?"

My mother sighs, more than a bit impatient. I know I'm eavesdropping — but there are lots of people around who can hear the conversation, it's hardly private.

"Look, I know you don't approve of me," Mom says. "But I moved to the city and I supported myself and I did the best I could. I wanted bigger, better things. For me and my daughter."

Mr. Belichek smiles, his eyes full of empathy. "Arlene, you know how much you love your daughter? That's exactly how much your mother loved you."

Mom doesn't have an answer for that. As a matter of fact, it makes her very emotional. I decide to step in — and she gives me a bright smile.

"Hey, Mom."

But I realize she's smiling at someone else. "Donny? Donny, is that you?"

Donny, shy as ever, gives her a small wave.

"After all these years, I can't believe it. You're still here. Donny, let's dance. I'm so bored — if I'm going to this Apple Whatever Festival, I might as well dance."

Fully expecting a warm welcome, she walks toward him reaching out — but he pulls back.

"I'm sorry, Arlene," he says. "But I've saved this dance for someone else."

I've hardly ever heard Donny speak that many words in a row, and I'm not the only one who is surprised. He walks over to Samantha, from the property tax office.

"Samantha, care to dance?"

Samantha is the most surprised of all. A beat, as everyone seems to freeze. Samantha meets the gaze of her old cheerleading teammate and says, "I would love to dance, Donny." As they walk to the dance floor past Mom, Samantha says, "Welcome back, Arlene. I guess some things have changed around here."

Rupert comes back out then, just as Mom is telling me, "Carly, I'm tired. I think I'm leaving."

Rupert takes notice of her, with her decidedly urban clothes and perfectly coiffed hair and makeup. "Well, hello!"

Mom notices Rupert's British accent and looks him over. "You're not from North Haven."

"No, I'm from London, but I live in Los Angeles much of the time."

"Mom, this is—"

But she speaks over me. "Darling, introduce me to this handsome gentleman!"

"This is Rupert, the director I've been telling you about."

Her whole manner changes, and so does his. They recognize something in each other — something that says they're both from the city, with careers and ambition and a subscription to *The New Yorker*.

"Ah yes, the director," she says, perhaps remembering that he fired me. "I'm Arlene." She bats her eyelashes, so I guess all is forgiven for him letting me go.

"And what do you do for a living, Arlene?"

"I'm an investment banker."

And they are off to the races, talking about everything from their careers to the best hotels in Santa Barbara.

Happy for the break, I wander around the Apple Blossom Festival by myself, soaking in the perfect evening. Some old men play horseshoes and some young girls make friendship bracelets. A group of moms with toddlers trade preschool recommendations and a gaggle of teen boys say "bro!" to each other over and over.

As the band strikes up another number, I see Donny pulling Samantha back onto the dance floor again. "This is our song!" he tells her.

"We have a song?" Samantha asks, but she's laughing like a kid and he spins her around. My heart swells seeing their love bloom before my eyes. Blossom Festival, indeed.

I spot Boone across the dance floor and head toward him. He's petting Rex and checking on the bee sting. Whit and Celia take Rex with them out on the dance floor, leaving the two of us alone. Or as alone as you can be at a street dance that the whole town attends.

"Hey, I'm glad to see you," I say.

"Rex's bee sting is all better."

"That's good."

I feel like it's on me to make amends, although I am

not exactly sure what I did wrong. But I know I want to connect with Boone. "Would you like to dance?" That sounds so forward, I think maybe I'm blushing. "Or I mean — if you want to?"

Boone doesn't crack a smile. "I love to dance. I took three years of tap and ballet."

"No preconceived notions."

He wraps his arm around my waist, and I gasp involuntarily. "Actually never had a lesson in my life," he says. "But if you believed a guy like me took ballet, my work here is done."

And he spins me out onto the dance floor. I don't know if I'm dizzy from the spin or just lightheaded from his presence. Whatever it is, it feels great.

We dance together naturally, comfortably. Boone never drops eye contact as we glide through the other dancers, and I feel my skirt blowing behind me as we go.

"You convince Rupert to rent the farm yet?" he says.

"No, but it's looking good."

"That's great." He smiles sadly. "Take some photos of the house before they paint it all white."

"Who knows, maybe they'll paint it pink. Or turquoise. You'll have to come see for yourself." I'm kidding around but he's not.

"I don't think I could stand to see those old timbers get destroyed. If I had a home like that, I'd lay down my life to defend it."

"You know, I really don't know what else you expect me to do. I've done my best."

"You're right. I'm being unreasonable I guess."

But now I'm revved up, so I continue, "First you don't want me to sell it because they'll tear it down and make the whole place a neighborhood of new houses. Then you don't want me to rent it because they'll paint it and cut down a few trees. You know, I can't stop things from changing."

"Really? I'm not sure how hard you're trying." He sighs, maybe a little aware that he's being overly demanding. "You have to understand, I've taken care of that place every day since your grandmother died. You show up after three years and throw your hands in the air."

"That's just not fair, Boone." We're barely dancing now, just swaying a little in the middle of the dance floor, barely aware that anyone's around us. "Can you tell me something?"

He nods.

"Why did you come find me in New York?" I ask.

"Because I wanted you to know that the place was okay, and that I was keeping it ready for you."

I don't have a reply to that.

Boone stops dancing completely. "I just know that if I had a chance like you have, I'd try harder."

A long beat as we lock eyes, the emotions charging between us. His looks like sadness, but mine is anger. How dare he!

"Boone, I'm sorry you don't have a family farm, but that's not my fault!"

That came out a little harsher than I meant it to. Okay,

122

a lot harsher, and I kind of regret it.

Boone nods. "You're right. I've overstepped. The place is yours to do with as you please."

"That's not what I meant."

"You know, I think I've fulfilled my promise to your grandmother. I don't think she ever dreamed you'd be tearing apart her house like this. But I said I'd help you and I did. From here on out, you're on your own, Carly."

We aren't dancing anymore, and in this moment it's like everyone around us has disappeared. Boone starts to pull away, but I grab the shirt on his chest with both hands,. "Wait."

"I'm sorry, Carly," he says, his voice cracking with emotion. "I can't watch it be torn apart. It's the closest thing to home I have left in this world."

And he walks away, leaving me alone on the dance floor.

The song ends, and I see Samantha and Donny practically floating back to their table. They call me over to say hi.

"You two are so cute out there together," I say.

They're full of love and laughter, inviting me to sit with them. A couple in love, and it makes me wish more than ever that Boone was still here. I am just not sure what he expects of me! But I shake it off.

Something occurs to me. "Samantha, remember when you were talking about nonprofit organizations? And how they don't have to pay property taxes, right?"

"Yes, sure," she tells me. "But the land has to be used for the public good. There's a whole application process."

I ask her a dozen more questions, and then a dozen more after that. As I go off in search of Boone, I see Irene and Doc Mullins on the edge of things, having a glass of apple cider at a picnic table.

"Do you know where Boone is?" I ask.

Irene gives me a warm smile. "Sure, hon. Just gave him the keys a little while ago — he's over at the office checking on the critters. Can't keep him out of there."

I nod my thanks, then say, "Actually, while I have you two here, can I ask you a couple questions?"

FIFTEEN

Mr. Belichek is setting up a big display of fireworks. I walk by him on my way to the vet's office and notice that Boone is helping him.

"Carly!" says Mr B. "We were just looking for you!"

It's clear Boone was not looking for me, by the look on his face.

"Can I help?" I say.

"I think we're all set. I know just how your granny liked her fireworks!" he says with a wink, making me wonder once again about his double meanings. I have to smile.

"It's a wonderful tribute to her," I say.

"I like to think she can see it. From the other side of the sky." He gets a little misty.

Boone and I glance at each other simultaneously, making eye contact, but both looking away quickly.

Mr. Belichek puts one arm around me and the other around Boone. "While I've got you two kids here, I want to say my piece."

Boone is looking at the ground, so I do too. I have no idea what's coming.

"Life's short. Times change, but we can't stay frozen in the past. I know both of you have been through a lot. Carly, growing up without a father and then losing your grandmother. Boone, your mama running off and then your father passing on."

I can feel the lump in my throat and I nod.

"Yes sir," says Boone in a whisper.

"But you can't stay stuck in that past. Don't let perfect be the enemy of good. When something worthwhile comes your way, you have to grab it."

"That's what I'm trying to do," I say.

And at that, Boone steps forward abruptly. "And I think you should," he says. And he starts walking down the street, away from the festival.

I'm shocked that he would just up and leave like this. It's downright rude, right in the middle of us all talking. I turn to Mr. Belichek and shake my head, as if to say, *Can you believe him?*

Mr. B says, "The fireworks don't start for half an hour."

I'm frozen in place, the wheels of my brain whirring like mad. A million possibilities flashing through my mind.

"Thanks!" I say and turn to run after Boone.

WHAT HAPPENED TO MY EX

* * *

He's already inside the vet's office because where else would this big-hearted man who loves animals retreat to? I find him in the back room, giving treats to various animals who are recuperating in their crates overnight.

"Hey, what are you doing?" I say.

He doesn't turn around. He obviously knows it's me. Who else would be stalking him in here?

"I come in and check on the animals sometimes. Doc likes the help," he says.

I walk down the row of cages, looking at the wide variety of puppies and cats and even a family of guinea pigs. "What's wrong with all of them?"

Boone shrugs. "Nothing, really. These are mostly just rescues that don't have homes."

That maybe sounds a little more meaningful than he meant it to, and he clears his throat.

"That's really sad," I say.

Boone keeps himself busy with the animals until I step in front of him, so he has to look at me.

"Because everyone needs a home."

He shakes his head. "Let's not do this. It's pointless."

"No, it's not! I'm really sorry."

"Yeah, it's fine." He turns back to a little puppy that's whining and slips a treat through the crate door. "You weren't wrong," he adds.

"I was wrong about me. I always thought I wanted to

help people make movies, but maybe I just want to help people. I don't really care about the Hollywood of it all. I want to…belong."

"What are you talking about?"

I take his hand. "Boone, will you come with me? Please? Trust me."

* * *

We find Mom and Rupert sitting at a table, drinking wine and discussing the best art house theaters in Manhattan. I pull Boone by the hand toward their table.

"Could we get another round?" Rupert says, not realizing it's us.

"Oh, it's Boone, the farmhand," says Mom. She seems a little tipsy, maybe from the wine or maybe from the attention of a man — something she's always enjoyed. She keeps her focus on Boone. "Thank you for helping Carly with the — oh, cleaning and such. I hope you can get your old horses out of there soon. Rupert was just saying they might want to shoot in the barn." She smiles at the director.

"Yes," Rupert says. "The crew will arrive soon and they take care of everything from here. Getting the place ready — painting, emptying it out. Because I require very specific things!"

"Let me guess. You need a working atmosphere that is more conducive to your creativity.'" I actually mimic his intonation a tiny bit.

"Excuse me?" Rupert seems genuinely surprised.

"Carly!" says Mom. "Don't be disrespectful."

But I don't think I am being disrespectful, I think I'm being honest. For once. "Rupert, I have to tell you something," I say. I gather my confidence. I'm feeling half scared and half cat-ate-the-canary. "Goodland Farm is no longer for rent."

"What?!" he says.

"WHAT?!" Mom says.

Several people look over at us now, to see what's going on. "I appreciate your interest, but we are no longer going to rent out Granny's house or land to a movie company."

Mom shrugs. "Well, then the county will take it for back taxes."

Boone takes my arm, pulls me up against him urgently. "Carly, you don't have to do this."

I push myself even closer against him. "I found a loophole in the paperwork," I say, brimming with the good news.

"Don't be foolish, Carly," says Mom. "Just rent the place to the film, and then you can sell it later for profit. It's better to get something than nothing."

"That's what I used to think, Mom." I thread my fingers through Boone's, facing the world side by side. "But I don't want anything unless it is true to me. I love North Haven. It might not be for you, but that doesn't mean it's not for me."

I look around and notice several people have gathered and are listening. I see Mr. Belichek, Samantha and Donny, Crystal the realtor, Whit and Celia with Rex, Irene and Doc Mullins.

I charge on. "I love the people here. Everyone believes in pitching in to help each other. And that's the way I want to live." I walk to my mom, kneeling down next to her. "Mom, I appreciate so much everything you've ever done for me. But I have to do this. I belong here."

The realization washes over her. And honestly, she doesn't even seem mad. "You always did follow your own north star, Carly. I love you. I always said I was bringing you up to be a strong, independent woman — and guess what." She laughs. "It looks like I did."

We hug, and I'm not the only one who sheds a tear. But we are both smiling too.

Rupert's not feeling the vibe though. "You bring me out here to this town in the middle of nowhere? And you practically beg me to rent your broken-down farm? And now you say it's not for rent?"

I stand to face him, nodding. "Apologies, Rupert. But it's not worth destroying the house — painting over the original wood, messing up Granny's old stove, cutting down the ancient elm trees."

"What am I supposed to do now?" he moans.

That's when Whit steps up and says, "I might know a place. My family owns some land on the edge of town with a huge old empty house on it. I can show it to you in the morning." Rex barks his approval.

WHAT HAPPENED TO MY EX

Mr. Belichek announces that it's time for the fireworks show, and the whole crowd meanders that way. I slip my arm through Boone's and he puts his other hand over mine. He smiles at me and it says a lot. As a matter of fact, no other smile in the history of mankind has been better or said more.

"I kind of can't believe I just did that," I said.

"Carly, are you sure you know what you're doing?" he says. "You're just delaying the inevitable. Silp-Co will probably do all of those same things — and then they will own it."

"No, listen. Let me explain — if the farm is a nonprofit, we don't have to pay property taxes. I talked to Samantha, and she verified everything."

"What are you talking about? We just push a button? How will that work?"

"I was thinking, what if we opened an animal rescue at Goodland Farm?"

He takes this in. I can almost hear things clicking into place in his brain. "An animal rescue?"

"Yes! I talked to Doc Mullins and Irene. There's a lot of funding out there if you apply for grants. For dogs and cats and horses. And raccoons." I smile but I'm serious. "To get them on their feet again. Give them a home."

We get to the open area where the fireworks will be. Boone stops and turns toward me. The soft moonlight is enough for us to see each other's eyes clearly, sparkling with excitement and nervousness.

"Boone, we could help so many animals, from all over southern Vermont."

"This might actually work, you think?"

"I majored in business, and I took a class on setting up nonprofits. It was a requirement, but I didn't think I would ever use it!" I laugh. "Turns out I kind of know how to form charitable corporations and apply for 501c3 status. I don't know why I didn't think of it before! Doc already wants to rent some space, and Samantha will help us apply for the grants. And Irene is going to help too."

"Carly, I don't want you to do this just to please anyone else. Especially not just to please me. Are you sure about it?"

I put my hands on his shoulders and he wraps his arms around my waist. "Nothing has ever felt more right," I say. "Ever since I've been in North Haven, things have felt like home. I didn't want to admit it — but I fit in here. I can't think of anything I'd rather do or any place I'd rather be."

Boone kisses me. I kiss Boone. We kiss each other. My heart skips a beat as he moves from my mouth, softly kissing across my cheek, winding up at my ear. "Me neither" he whispers, and kisses my neck.

The feedback from the microphone on the bandstand screeches, and all eyes turn that way, including ours.

It's Mr. Belichek, making an announcement. "Everyone, the fireworks are about to begin! But first, I just heard something from Doc Mullins that I'd like to share. Congratulations to Carly Walton and Boone Akers, who are starting a much-needed animal rescue out at Goodland Farm!"

There's applause through the crowd. Boone looks at me like, *How did Mr. B know that?* And I whisper, "News travels fast in North Haven."

Mr. Belichek continues, "And I'd like to pledge the first donation! An animal shelter is something we've needed in this area for a long, long time. There could be no better cause. And no better people to run it!"

As the townspeople are saying "hear, hear!" the fireworks begin.

The exploding balls of sparks illuminate all of us, with our smiling faces turned upward.

"Are we really doing this?" says Boone.

"I think we really are."

We lean into each other, gazing at the exploding lights overhead. It's so incredibly romantic.

"One time," I tell Boone, "I saw a flock of ducks flying through something like this."

He's immediately concerned. "Were they hurt?"

"Oh no, they were fire-quackers."

He nods, not reacting. I, however, cannot hold back my laugh.

"Carly, do your legs hurt? After the long way you went for that joke?"

"I'm so sorry." I can't stop giggling. "That was bad."

"I guess you just have a flare for humor."

I groan. "Okay, we have to stop."

"You started it!"

"You mean I ignited it."

We are both laughing, giddy in this moment. Alive for each other. He turns away from the fireworks, locking eyes with me. "What you're doing is a good thing."

"What we're doing."

"Your granny would be so proud."

That puts a knot in my throat. "You know, I realize that all I ever wanted to do was help people. And by people, I mean animals of course."

"Of course."

"And maybe a few people too. I'm thinking there are a lot strays out there, just like us, who could use a real home."

"I resemble that remark," he says.

I can't stop smiling even as our faces get closer. "Everyone needs a place to put down roots."

"And to remember where they're from."

The grand finale of the fireworks above us. The ground of home below us. The love between us.

Boone and I kiss like we've never kissed before. Like we will forever.

THANKS SO MUCH FOR READING!

WHATEVER HAPPENED TO MY EX is part of The Heartfelt Romantic Comedy Series.

These stand-alone contemporary romances can be read in any order and are available on Kindle Unlimited.

If you're so inclined, leave a review on Amazon or on Goodreads .

Your voice has the power to lift up a book!

Hope to see you in North Haven again soon x

A FEEL-GOOD FESTIVE ROMCOM!
A QUICK, WITTY READ FULL OF WINTER FUN.

Available Now

COMING JULY 7, 2023

Pre-Order Now

Made in the USA
Coppell, TX
15 August 2024

36005632R00083